CW00847598

CLARITY JONES
AND THE
MAGICAL
DETECTIVE
AGENCY

Chris Smith is an author, broadcaster and former champion bellringer (true story). For many years he worked as a newsreader and co-host on radio stations including Xfm and BBC Radio 1 before dreaming up Kid Normal *with his radio husband at the time, Greg James, in 2017. He published his first solo book,* Frankie Best Hates Quests, *in 2022.*

Chris divides his time between his house in London and an imaginary land filled with odd creatures where anything can happen. He enjoys playing the guitar, travelling, running, climbing mountains and eating cheese but not all at the same time.

Books by Chris Smith:

Frankie Best Hates Quests

Books by Chris Smith, with Greg James:

Kid Normal

Kid Normal and the Rogue Heroes

Kid Normal and the Shadow Machine

Kid Normal and the Final Five

The Great Dream Robbery

Super Ghost

Follow Chris on social media

 @itschrissmith

 @chrissmithstagram

CLARITY JONES

AND THE

MAGICAL DETECTIVE AGENCY

CHRIS SMITH

Illustrated by
KENNETH ANDERSON

PUFFIN

PUFFIN BOOKS
UK | USA | Canada | Ireland | Australia
India | New Zealand | South Africa

Puffin Books is part of the Penguin Random House group of companies
whose addresses can be found at global.penguinrandomhouse.com.

www.penguin.co.uk   www.puffin.co.uk   www.ladybird.co.uk

First published 2023

001

Text copyright © Chris Smith, 2023
Illustrations copyright © Kenneth Anderson, 2023

The moral right of the author and illustrator has been asserted

Text design by Anita Mangan

Printed and bound in Great Britain by Clays Ltd, Elcograf S.p.A.

The authorized representative in the EEA is Penguin Random House Ireland,
Morrison Chambers, 32 Nassau Street, Dublin D02 YH68

A CIP catalogue record for this book is available from the British Library

ISBN: 978–0–241–52213–4

All correspondence to:

Puffin Books, Penguin Random House Children's
One Embassy Gardens, 8 Viaduct Gardens
London SW11 7BW

This book is dedicated to two of my teachers:

Mr Cotter, who read us The Hobbit.

And Mrs Lawman, who gave me an entry form for a story competition and said 'this is for you.' Turns out she was right.

When you have eliminated all which is impossible, then whatever remains, however improbable, must be the truth.

Sherlock Holmes

Never eliminate the impossible.

Clarity Jones

Watchtowers

DRACONIAN
WASTES

North Gate

MAGES'
QUARTER

The
CASTLE

Knights'
Academy

Oxbow Moat

ASSASSINS'
QUARTER

Cause-
way

Strangers'
Tower

MERCHANTS'
QUARTER

Merchants'
Bazaar

RIVER RILL

Wharves

Oxenbridge

Bridge
of
Tears

THE GREAT
CITY of
MEANDERMART

Bone Way

Corth-way

Graveyard

FLYGER MOUNTAINS

The wizard had been murdered. To a trained eye, the signs were unmistakable. See if you can untangle any of these clues for yourself.

First clue: there was clear evidence that somebody had forced their way in. The thick wooden front door of the tall, rickety house where the wizard lived had been kicked right down. It had been left lying flat on the floor, with a large muddy footprint clearly visible right in the middle of it.

Second clue: a keen observer might have noticed that somebody had been making threats against the wizard. To one side of his cluttered front room there was a desk piled high with the usual wizardly nonsense: tall green glass phials, dusty old books with words written in a language that looked like Latin but wasn't, a few odd-coloured crystals . . . you know the kind of stuff. Anyway, on this desk, half tucked underneath a feather duster, was a large sheet of parchment with the words

You will die, Wizard!
Korg the Destroyer

picked out in elaborate gothic script in neat black ink. Significant.

Third clue (and perhaps the most telling of all, if you really know what you're looking for): the wizard's head had been cut clean off. Most of him was spreadeagled on the stone floor, legs splayed as if he'd been running away from the door. His head, however, was not in its traditional position on top of his shoulders. Instead, it had been placed on the mantelpiece, from where it overlooked the untidy room wearing a floppy blue hat with moons on it and a startled expression.

Yes, the clues were all there if you knew where to look for them. The wizard had been murdered. Even the Meandermart City Watch managed to work that out, and, as you're about to discover, the guards of the Meandermart City Watch are not *generally* selected for their dazzling intelligence.

'Someone's done murdered that wizard,' grunted the armoured woman who walked past in the early hours of the morning during her patrol of the cramped and dingy corner of Meandermart known as the Mages' Quarter.

'What, another one?' grumbled her deputy, a shorter man who had to crane his neck to peer over her shoulder. 'Yep,' he confirmed mournfully. 'You got it in one, Captain. That one's been right killed. Head clean off and everything.'

'He's dead all right,' agreed the Watch Captain. 'Head off,' she repeated, nodding to herself. 'That'll do it for you.' Holding her flaming torch above her head, she leaned into the room and looked around. Dawn was only just breaking, and a pale light cast thick shadows around the room that flickered and jumped in the orange firelight. 'Hmm, look over there.' Stepping carefully, she moved to the table and examined the parchment, her lips moving soundlessly as she spelled out the message. '"You will die, Wizard!" it says here,' she called back to her companion after a few moments.

'Hmm. Do *sound* like someone be threatening him,' observed the deputy guard with a sage nod, reaching under his tarnished helmet to scratch his hair. (They're very itchy, helmets.)

'Reckon you're right,' his boss agreed. 'It's signed "Korg the Destroyer",' she went on slowly.

'You know what *I* think happened here?' Her deputy sounded excited as he stepped into the room behind her. 'I reckon this Korg the Destroyer, whoever he is, I reckon he done murdered that there wizard. And the method of the murderin' that was done,' he concluded, holding up a stubby yet triumphant finger, 'was the a-cuttin' off of that there head what has been placed atop the mantel yonder.'

'And you know what *I* think?' countered his boss. 'I reckon we did done solve this here murder!' A delighted grin spread across the deputy's face. 'I spotted all the clues, I did.' The deputy's grin vanished as he realized that he wasn't going to get any credit for his clue-spotting. 'Now,' the watch captain went on, rubbing her hands together, 'all we needs to do is track down this Korg the Destroyer person and arrest them. Then we can be back in the castle in time to sling them in the dungeons before breakfast.'

The deputy guard's grin reappeared faintly. It's hard not to cheer up when someone mentions breakfast.

'I wonder where Korg the Destroyer do be?' he pondered out loud, turning to look up and down the deserted street outside. 'They sound scary,' he admitted quietly. 'What if they come back?' His hand tightened round the hilt of his sword.

Just then there came a splashing, pattering sound from somewhere away to the right – the sound of footsteps in the mud. The guard stepped out from the doorway, adjusting his helmet and fumbling for his sword, getting his hand tangled up in his cloak in the process. 'Halt!' he shouted hoarsely. 'Be identifyin' of yourself!' Nightmare visions of a horrific monster called Korg the Destroyer flitted through his mind as the footsteps came closer. A flickering shadow grew on the whitewashed walls of the tightly packed houses.

But what came round the corner in the softly growing early-morning light was not any kind of monster. It was something less terrifying but equally strange. It was a wooden chest, its curved lid bound with thick straps of iron. And the wooden chest was trotting down the street towards the wizard's house on four short, stout wooden legs.

The City Watch guard had seen wooden chests before. He even had a very nice one at home, in which he kept precious things like money and cheese. But he had never seen a walking chest before. It was such an odd sight that it completely robbed him of the power of intelligent speech. Not that his speech up till then had been particularly intelligent, but you know.

'Fleeeh,' garbled the guard as the wooden chest approached him, giving a skittish little leap like an excited dog. 'Beff. Phwaaarp.'

'Why do you be sayin' "fleeeh, beff, phwaaarp"?' asked the Watch Captain, coming back to the door of the wizard's house and holding up her torch again.

'Pweeeep,' he explained, pointing to the wooden chest on legs, which had now stopped in front of them and was emitting a faint panting noise.

'Greaalp!' gurgled his boss, taking a short leap backwards and almost tripping over the eighty-five per cent of the wizard that had been left on the floor.

'Smyll!' came a voice from down the street. 'Where are you, boy? What have you found?' And, as the two guards of the City Watch watched in the same way they did most things – that is to say, dumbly – three figures strode into view out of the haze. It was very dramatic and should really have been accompanied by some quite stirring music. In fact, it was accompanied by the sound of someone further down the street emptying their chamber pot out of their window, but let's gloss over that for now as it'll spoil the moment. Let's focus. The main characters of this story are about to appear and we don't want to get distracted by the sound – or indeed the smell – of a chamber pot.

The three figures were advancing along the street, which was made of compacted soil with the odd paving stone placed here and there in front of some of the nicer houses. Leading the trio was a tall woman dressed in a deep blue cloak. She had long, flowing hair that reached all the way down her back.

She wore high boots and a thick leather belt, and had calm, watchful eyes that moved from one side to the other constantly as she strode towards the guards. At her side, stepping sideways in order to cast frequent, watchful glances behind her, was a small, slight girl dressed from head to toe in black leather. Her eyes were narrowed and full of suspicion, and she moved in a slight crouch, as if constantly ready to spring into action. And behind them both, attempting to pick a way between the muddiest patches of the street, was a hulking figure coated in shaggy white fur. It was fully eight feet tall, and its yellow eyes burned angrily.

'I absolutely hate coming out when it's been raining,' the enormous creature was saying crossly to the woman in the cloak. 'Look at this!' It hopped for a few steps, holding up its other foot and pointing to it with a claw. 'Completely filthy!' The leg was indeed caked in mud almost up to the knee. And the knee, remember, was the height of most people's waists. 'I'll have to wait until this dries and then comb it out! Can you even *begin* to imagine how painful that's going to be?' Tutting crossly, it stepped gingerly on to one of the paving stones, which pivoted unexpectedly, sending a plume of filthy water jetting upward. The white-furred monster howled in frustration. 'It's going to be completely impossible to clean this all off!' it wailed.

The tall woman stopped in front of the wizard's house, a slight smile on her face as she turned back towards her tall companion. 'Impossible?' she echoed quietly, raising a quizzical eyebrow.

'You know what I mean.' The huge feet squelched as the gigantic figure stumped down the street to join her. 'This'd better be worth it,' it muttered darkly, wiping its muddy legs ineffectually with a large, clawed hand.

The two guards of the City Watch had been observing this exchange with their mouths hanging open. The deputy was still gawping at the wooden chest on legs; his boss was now pointing with a shaking finger at the huge shape looming above her. 'Monster,' she husked hoarsely. 'It's a monster!'

'Rude,' countered the creature in its deep, rumbling voice. 'Never seen a snow gnoblin before?' Eyes wide, the guard shook her head.

At this point, the blue-cloaked woman broke into this exchange, calling, 'Good morning, friends,' and giving the two guards a friendly smile. 'My helper there, Smyll, seems to have sniffed out a mystery.' She gestured towards the wooden chest, which was now using one of its legs to point inside the wizard's house and emitting a slight jingling sound as it quivered with excitement. 'We're here to help,' the woman went on in a reassuring tone.

'And just who might you be?' asked the captain sternly, wiggling the hilt of her sword in what she vainly hoped was an intimidating fashion.

'Clarity Jones, M.I.,' replied the woman confidently. 'That's Magical Investigator,' she added, leaning forward and lowering her voice slightly. 'I'm a detective.'

'What in the name of all three of the Three Kingdoms is a "detective"?' responded the guard with a mixture of scorn and confusion. Scorfusion, you might call it if you're short of time and can only digest one word.

'A detective,' explained Clarity Jones, 'is somebody that detects things. You know –' she waved her hands in a circular motion – 'when something *strange* has happened, a detective works out what's gone on. Detect the truth – detect – detective. Get it?'

The Watch Captain screwed up her face in an even more extreme display of scorfusion. **'Whaaaaat?'** she screeched. 'What in all of Rillia do you be going on about?'

Now, a few questions might be occurring to you at this point, perhaps along the lines of: 'Where is Rillia?', 'What are the Three Kingdoms?' and 'Why has nobody heard the word "detective" before?' So perhaps a brief explanation is in order. Oh look, here comes one now! That was lucky.

A BRIEF EXPLANATION

We find ourselves in the great city of Meandermart, the easternmost city of the kingdom of Rillia. Rillia was one of three neighbouring countries known as the Three Kingdoms, for the simple reason that there were three of them. (Spess and Informatia were the names of the other two, if you're interested.) Meandermart was a great trading centre. It lay alongside the wide, slow waters of the River Rill, watched over by the castle that sat on a high hill right in the centre of the city. The castle features heavily in this story but not just yet. Be patient.

Anyway, why did nobody in Meandermart, or indeed in Rillia, or indeed in any of the Three Kingdoms, know what a detective is? For the simple reason that there had never been one there before. There were many career options available to the inhabitants of the Three Kingdoms. You could be a wizard, doing strange things with potions and incantations. You could be a guard of the City Watch. You could be a duke or duchess, as long as you were born in the right place at the right time. Or you could choose any of the professions you usually find in this kind of kingdom: rustic villager, plump jolly innkeeper, assassin, ranger, mud-caked hermit, knight, barbarian, mysterious person in the corner of an inn who presents the hero with a side quest . . . you know the kind of thing. But not a detective. Not until then. Clarity Jones was very much a trailblazer in that regard. She had decided to become the very first solver of mysteries, and had invented the word 'detective' to describe her chosen career in a format that was both snappy and easily understood. To her slight frustration, however, it was proving a little slow to catch on.

'Dect-ecter-ist?' queried the deputy guard, screwing up his face around the unfamiliar sounds.

'De-,' enunciated Clarity Jones carefully, 'tect-ive. My friends and I,' she went on, hoping to make things clearer and thinking to herself that she'd get better at this speech as time went on, 'are the Magical Detective Agency. We solve mysteries. And this morning we're here to solve –' she stood up on the toes of her high boots to look over the guard's shoulder – 'the Mystery of the Mage on the Mantelpiece.'

'Good title,' said the girl in black leather approvingly. She had been circling around on cat-like feet at the back of the group, casting suspicious glances left and right along the street and up at the rooftops above. 'Looks like a good mystery,' she added, peering through the doorway.

'There ain't no mystery 'ere to be solved!' burst out the City Watch boss. 'We done solved it already,' she went on proudly, puffing out her chest. 'That there wizard was murdered by Korg the Destroyer.'

'There's a note and everything,' added the other guard. 'Open and shut. Nothing else to say.'

'I see,' replied Clarity Jones in a level tone of voice.

It was best not to antagonize the City Watch. (To her way of thinking, the combination of large weapons and small brains was usually a dangerous one.) 'And have you asked Korg the Destroyer about this?'

'And how,' snapped the captain, 'would we do that? We don't even know where he lives!'

'Well, I don't want to teach you your job,' said Clarity gently. 'But do you think he might live over there?' She pointed to the other side of the street, where a large wooden sign above the door read:

Home of
Korg the Destroyer

'Well, it's very easy to be all *clever* about it,' huffed the captain, marching over the road and hammering on the door, bellowing 'OPEN UP IN THE NAME OF THE CITY WATCH!' in a needlessly loud voice. There was a scuffling and a scraping of bolts behind the door and it creaked open. For a moment it looked like there was nobody there, but when everybody looked down slightly they saw a tiny, stooped old man standing in the doorway. He had a pair of thick glasses balanced on his nose, which was large and criss-crossed with red veins.

'Yes?' he fluted in a high, quavery voice. 'Korg the Destroyer at your service. How can I help you this fine morning?'

'Did you cut yon wizard's head off?' demanded the captain, gesturing curtly back across the street.

'Oh dear,' said Korg the Destroyer, peering past the Magical Detective Agents and catching sight of the wizard's head on the mantelpiece. **'Poor old Prookin!'** he quavered, leaning against his door frame and pressing a hand to his forehead. 'That looks very nasty. Oh dear, very nasty indeed.'

'Did you do it?' she repeated, grabbing the hilt of her sword and wiggling it for emphasis.

'Of course he didn't do it, you idiot!' snapped the girl in black leather, losing her patience. She sidestepped towards them, gesturing angrily. 'Look at him! He couldn't reach that wizard's neck, let alone cut off his head! He looks like he'd run out of energy just crossing the street. How do you think he kicked the door in?'

'Well, why's he called a destroyer, then?' countered the deputy guard, unwilling to dismiss their nice, tidy murder-solving theory quite so easily.

'Well, in this magic business, being a mage – it's all

CLARITY JONES AND THE MAGICAL DETECTIVE AGENCY

about image, you know,' said the tiny old man apologetically. 'I used to be plain old Korg, but since I added "the Destroyer" part, I've had *so* much more interest.' Thus proving that even though the inhabitants of Rillia had been unfamiliar with the concept of a detective, they did have a firm grasp of the concept of branding. Korg pointed a shaking finger to the smaller sign beside his door, which read as follows:

KORG THE DESTROYER
ALL MAGE AND WIZARDING SERVICES CONSIDERED.
WEAPONS ENCHANTED, POTIONS CONCOCTED.
STRIKE FEAR INTO THE HEARTS OF YOUR ENEMIES!

'Thanks for your time, Mr Korg,' said Clarity Jones kindly. 'We'll call again if we need you.'

'Don't leave town in the meantime,' added the captain of the City Watch threateningly, in a vain attempt to stay in charge of the situation.

'Leave town?' muttered the leather-clad girl, shaking her head. **'He looks like he'd keel over if he tried to leave a chair!'**

'Right,' said Clarity decisively. 'Let's have a proper

look at the crime scene, shall we?' She recrossed the street, clicking her fingers. The wooden chest, which had been waiting patiently, sitting back on its haunches, now leaped into life and followed her into the wizard's house. It stopped just inside the doorway and, with a click, its lid flipped open to reveal a neat array of different-coloured jars, bottles and wooden boxes. The first-ever detective in all of Rillia looked around, feeling – as she did every time she encountered a mystery – a flutter of excitement in her tummy. She took in the door with the footprint planted on it. She read the note on the cluttered desk. She looked at the wizard's head on the mantelpiece. And she nodded to herself. 'Well,' said Clarity Jones, 'let's see if we can detect what happened here.'

'*Detect*,' said the huge shaggy white creature to the guards. 'Get it now?' But they both shook their heads.

'Smyll,' said Clarity Jones, clicking her fingers. And like a dog that's just heard the word 'walkies', the wooden chest gave a little jump and trotted over, the bottles and wooden boxes packed inside jiggling excitedly. 'Let's see about this note first of all, shall we?' continued Clarity. 'Something about it doesn't seem right.'

'**It's obvious!**' exclaimed the deputy guard from the doorway.

'Yes,' agreed Clarity Jones, 'that's probably it.' Bending down, she plucked a small silver disc from a slot on one side of the chest. As she waved it close to the note signed 'Korg the Destroyer', a vague design appeared on the disc – the shape of a fish began to form, outlined in faint red lines. 'As I thought,' said Clarity Jones in a satisfied tone. 'Red herring.'

'What in the Three Kingdoms be *that*?' demanded the guard, pointing at the disc.

'A misleader reader,' the detective explained. 'It tells me when something's designed to throw me off the scent. Right, let's hear what really happened, shall we?'

'What be she going to do?' said the senior guard to her deputy. 'Ask the walls whether they did see anything suspicious?' She elbowed her colleague in the ribs and they both chuckled at this fine witticism.

'Don't be ridiculous,' Clarity Jones told them. 'I'd never ask the walls. They're much too thick to be of any help.'

'They're not that thick,' replied a muffled voice from next door.

'I'll ask a chair,' declared Clarity. **'Witness powder please, Smyll!'** And, as the guards' laughter dried up like a puddle in a heatwave, Clarity bent down once again to the wooden chest and selected a box full of bright orange powder. Straightening up, she looked around the room once again. 'That looks like a good viewpoint,' she decided, striding over to a wooden chair that stood in the opposite corner. And, taking a generous pinch of the powder, she sprinkled it carefully all over the chair, paying particular attention to the high back where an elaborate pattern was carved into the dark, polished wood.

'What's she doing?' asked the City Watch woman suspiciously.

'Finding a witness,' explained the girl in black leather over her shoulder. She was standing with her back to the room, casting more watchful glances up and down the street and toying with a long, slim dagger that she seemed to have pulled from the complicated hair braid on top of her head.

A strange sound filled the wizard's house – a long, deep creaking like very old timbers being bent and contorted. And, as the sound turned into a huge yawn, the chair flexed its arms and legs like someone stretching after a satisfying sleep. The carved area at the top of its back began to move and swirl, two lines raising like eyebrows. And, beneath them, two deep green eyes opened sleepily. 'Who's there?' grumbled the chair in a croaky, grumpy voice.

'I'm very sorry to wake you,' said the detective in the blue cloak politely. 'My name's Clarity Jones, and I'm a . . .' She hesitated. The witness powder wouldn't last long, and she didn't want to waste time explaining what a detective was all over again. 'I've got some quick questions for you,' she said. 'It won't take long.'

'I'm so tired,' the chair complained, closing its eyes again.

'Just very quickly,' urged Clarity. Behind her, the guards of the City Watch were gawping in amazement. 'The wizard who lives in this house . . .' Clarity went on.

'Oh yes, *him*,' said the chair moodily. 'Always sitting on me, he is.'

'Somebody's cut his head off,' broke in the girl in black leather, moving across to stand at Clarity's shoulder.

'I know.' There was a hint of smugness in the chair's voice now. 'Might make him a bit lighter, at any rate.' (OK, the chair isn't coming across as a very sympathetic character, but just think for a moment about what a chair's life is like. Nothing but bottoms, all day long, and never a word of thanks. It's enough to make anyone slightly grumpy.)

'Did you see who did it?' asked Clarity loudly. Already the carvings on the chair's back were moving more sluggishly.

'Were it Korg the Destroyer from over the road?' bellowed the Watch Captain, still desperate to take the credit for solving the murder. Clarity frantically shushed her with a hand, but it was too late.

'The little tiny man?' said the chair through another huge yawn. 'Oh . . . no. This person was much bigger. Kicked the door right down, he did. Makes me tired just thinking about it. So . . . tired.' And, with that, the carved eyes closed and the chair went back to being a chair.

'Wake it up again!' urged the deputy. 'That were brilliant! Wait till I tells the wife about this! Talking chairs? I never seen the like!'

'Silence!' hissed the black-clad girl, adding the words 'you fool' under her breath.

'What is that stuff, anyway?' asked the captain.

'Proper magical, that is! Not like most of the stuff they peddle round here.'

'Witness powder,' said Clarity Jones, snapping the box full of orange powder shut and kneeling to replace it neatly inside the wooden chest on legs. 'Very, very rare. Allows me to question the furniture. But it can only be used once at each crime scene, and it doesn't last very long.'

'Which is why it's extremely important that she's not interrupted while she's working,' went on the girl in black leather, shooting the guard a look that, if looks could kill, would have run her through with an icicle. (Luckily for her, looks *can't* kill. Not unless you run into the very rare and dangerous pharmodrile, a lizard-like creature that weeps tears of a powerful poison. But that's another story.)

'Well, we found something out, at least,' said Clarity with a sigh, getting to her feet. She had a small phial of blue glass in her hand. 'The chair told us that whoever kicked in the door is also the killer. And they left us a very convenient footprint.' She walked to the wooden door and uncorked the phial. 'Let's see what the blue print has to tell us.'

'Is the footprint going to wake up and start tellin''

us what 'appened?' asked the guard captain, her knees clicking as she crouched down in anticipation.

'Not quite,' said Clarity. 'Ready, Mirko? Ready, Nissassa?' The hulking, white-furred beast and the girl in black nodded. 'Right, then.' Carefully, she dripped a liquid from the phial on to the footprint. At once, it began to glow a soft blue colour. And after that, more blue footprints appeared, leading backwards away from the door, out of the doorway and back down the street.

'Aha! Looks like we've found a trail to follow,' said Clarity Jones. She nodded to the two guards. 'I'll let you take it from here,' she said, gesturing to one part of the wizard with her left hand and the other part with her right. 'Don't go throwing Korg in the dungeons now, will you?' she warned them. 'We've shown you he's innocent. The Magical Detective Agents will be back soon with the real killer. The game's afoot! Let's go!' And with a swish of cloak, a jingle of concealed weaponry and the stump of furry feet in the mud, Clarity, Nissassa and Mirko swept out of the door and away, following the backwards trail of blue-glowing footprints as it led them rapidly down the street.

The Watch Captain scratched her head. 'Well, I don't know about you,' she said, sinking down on to the chair that had proved such an unexpected witness to the wizard's murder. 'But I've got no idea who that was.'

'That were Meandermart's greatest dretectint, that were,' replied her deputy wonderingly, gazing down the street after Clarity and her two crime fighters as they vanished round a corner with the wooden chest scampering after them.

'Well, that's the part I don't understand,' his boss complained. 'I still don't get it. What's a destectiver?'

Meanwhile, elsewhere in the Mages' Quarter, a small, weasel-faced man was just handing over a jingling pouch of gold to a large man with a sword fastened to his belt. 'So, you're sure he's dead?' the little man asked in a thin, reedy voice.

'I cut his 'ead orf,' grunted the other. 'That usually tends to do the trick.'

'And you're certain you got away with it?' asked the weaselly man, glancing nervously towards the door. 'Nobody could have possibly followed you?' His eyes darted back to a table that stood to one side of the room, where a large and very old-looking book sat. 'The City Watch didn't see you?'

'Those idiots?' said the large man scornfully. 'They don't see past the ends of their noses. No, you're in the clear, my friend. The mage is dead; you got his magic book; the blame's been pinned on his neighbour; and nobody will ever find out it was really you.'

Unfortunately for the weasel-faced man, exactly fifty per cent of the previous four statements were entirely untrue. And this was proved by the sound that came next: running feet outside the door. As the little man looked in horror, a line of glowing blue footprints appeared on the floor of his house, leading directly to the boots of the man with the sword. And before they could say, 'Why has that line of glowing footprints appeared?' the door was suddenly torn off its hinges by a gigantic creature with white fur.

'Ouch,' said the creature. 'I think I got a splinter. If I start bleeding into my fur, I'm going to be absolutely furious. Blood's impossible to shift.'

'*You* are responsible for cutting off a mage's head,' announced Clarity Jones, striding into the room with her eyes on the blue glowing footprints and pointing at the sword-carrying man. His hand immediately went to the hilt of his weapon, but a somersaulting figure in black jumped neatly over Clarity's shoulder and held a slim blade to his throat.

'I wouldn't do that if I were you,' warned Nissassa.

'Mirko, take them both to the City Watch,' instructed Clarity.

'They don't look very clean,' grumbled the snow gnoblin as he gathered up the two men like bundles of clothes, tucking one under each arm.

'Why did they kill that mage?' wondered Nissassa, replacing the dagger in her high boot.

'Let's find out, shall we?' replied Clarity, clicking her fingers again. There was a clonking and jangling as Smyll, the wooden chest, raced excitedly into the room, throwing its lid open with a happy creak. Clarity selected a tub of powder labelled

Loca-Motive

and, taking a pinch, blew it out in front of her. Immediately, the leather book on the table began to jiggle slightly. 'Looks like we located our motive,' said the detective in a satisfied tone, picking it up and leafing through the pages. It wasn't unusual for mages to have each other murdered in order to steal books of magic from each other. Real magic was extremely rare, after all. 'Doesn't even look genuine,' said Clarity. 'Ah well.' She closed the book with a snap. 'Case closed anyway. Back to base, Nissassa.'

And that, in short, was the Mystery of the Mage on the Mantelpiece. In many ways, like the book of magic on the table, it was very much open and shut. But a few weeks later, Clarity Jones and her friends embarked on a case that was to become famous throughout all of the Three Kingdoms. A case that also saw her detective agency gain a brand-new member. His name was Mutt, and he was eleven years old. And, in his whole short life, he'd never dreamed of being a detective. Because, like everyone else in Meandermart, he had absolutely *no* idea what a detective was. And that's where we'll start our story properly. It's time for Chapter 1. Ready?

CHAPTER 1

THE LOST BOY

May you find what you need, not what you seek.

Traditional Rillian farewell

Mutt was lost, Mutt was hungry, Mutt was alone.

Nothing very unusual about two thirds of that sentence; Mutt was always alone and he was usually hungry. But he had never, ever been lost before. Not until today. He looked around at the unfamiliar alleyway, panic hovering at the edge of his brain like the roar of a distant crowd. Where was he? In all his years of wandering the streets of Meandermart, he'd never got lost before. He knew the city like the back of his hand. Better, in fact (he wasn't the sort of boy who sat around staring at the back of his hand). He knew his way around the great city of Meandermart as well as he knew the number of pies in the goat-pie man's shop window. And he knew that exactly. There were thirty-seven of them.

'There he is!' With a porridgey splat of boots on the muddy ground (when you're as hungry as Mutt was, everything starts to sound like food), a group of people rounded the corner. They were about Mutt's age, but whereas he was undernourished, filthy and scrawny, they were well fed, well scrubbed and hefty. Built for chasing. Mutt, luckily, was built for running away. So, without hesitation, that's exactly what he did, taking off in the opposite direction in his bare feet, zigzagging down the winding streets like a fleeing hare, eyes wide and arms pumping as the hunting party thundered behind in pursuit.

It all sounds very dramatic, doesn't it, but in all honesty this was shaping up to be pretty much a typical Tuesday.

This particular Tuesday had started several hours before, with Mutt standing patiently outside the great eastern gates of the city as dawn picked out the clouds with streaks of watercolour orange. The winding, potholed road leading up to the gate was almost empty, with just a couple of farmers' wagons waiting to enter. Mutt could see the breath from the oxen that pulled the carts steaming in the chilly air – it was, after all, only a couple of weeks until the exact middle of winter, which would be marked by the great and very miserable holiday known as Moaningtide. Eventually, with much grinding and clanking, the gates swung slowly inwards to reveal a wide street sloping gently uphill towards the castle, perched high on its hill and still veiled in morning mist. Somewhere a ragged horn sounded to signal that the great city was ready to begin another day. The farmers shook the reins to urge their lumbering oxen on, and Mutt waited for them to pass before he slipped inside.

*M*OANINGTIDE is celebrated on the day that falls in the precise centre of winter. It is a day specially set aside to complain endlessly about the cold, damp weather and the long hours of darkness. For centuries, Rillians have commiserated Moaningtide with the singing of gripes and a special feast held during the brief hours of daylight on the shortest day. Family and friends gather round to exchange reasons why they are so very miserable and to point out to each other that spring is still months away. It's one of the most depressing holidays you can possibly imagine.

Instead of following the carts down the main street, Mutt immediately ducked left down a narrow alleyway and began to wind his way through the city towards the great river that flowed along its southern edge. As we know already, Mutt knew the back streets of Meandermart intimately. He knew the four main streets too – those wide streets that radiated out from the hill in the city centre like the spokes of a wheel. He knew the streets that linked them, the narrower, cluttered roads lined with houses and shops. And best of all he knew the winding paths that wove the city together like veins – the small streets the locals called gannicks, and the even smaller ways known as jitties that wound round the city, bending back upon themselves and linking up with each other in a bewildering maze like street spaghetti. It was easy to get lost in these parts of Meandermart. But not for Mutt. Without thinking, he weaved his way towards the river, turning left and right down gannicks, keeping the castle looming high above him to the right. Not many people were about – just a few early risers who eyed him suspiciously, and once or twice he caught sight of a gnanger returning to its burrow after its night's feasting.

GNANGERS are small, scaly creatures distantly related to the dragons that inhabit the Draconian Wastes to the north of Rillia. Gnangers are nocturnal and omnivorous, meaning that during the night they roam the streets of cities such as Meandermart, eating any refuse. Gnangers have extremely strong teeth, so they are able to chew up almost any substance. Rillians are now in the habit of simply throwing their household waste on to the streets at sundown, knowing it will have been eaten by dawn. Gnangers may just be the most useful creature you will ever encounter.

The streets around the Merchants' Quarter in south Meandermart were much busier; most wagons arrived from the south and trundled over the great stone structure of the Oxenbridge into the city. The smartly dressed Meandermartins hardly noticed Mutt as he dodged through the crowds, working his way towards the wide stone street that ran alongside the river, with the shops and stalls of the Merchants' Bazaar clustered along its northern edge. The air began to fill with the smell of cooking as he grew closer, and the masts of the ships tied up at the wharves speared the sky above him.

The ships that were tied up at Meandermart's docks and the wagons that rolled across the Oxenbridge brought goods from right across the Three Kingdoms and even, sometimes, from the lands beyond. At the stalls of the Merchants' Bazaar you could buy pretty much anything you could imagine – rich cloths woven in Spess to the south, rare books from Informatia, or swords and armour forged in the Twin Cities far to the east. Mutt passed a table laden with fresh vegetables and paused in front of a shop boasting 'REAL magic artefacts! Best prices!' He snorted. There wasn't much magic left – everybody knew that. And the few rare magical items that remained were guarded jealously by their owners – they certainly wouldn't be on sale here. Next to the magic shop was a smaller store selling lifna, the small, carved wooden figures that Rillians traditionally gave to each other at funerals. When someone died, a lifna would sit on the mantelpiece in the house where they'd lived, watching over those they'd left behind. Mutt passed quickly by and walked on, blinking.

Right in the centre of the bustling market, occupying a prime position opposite the largest wharf, where the biggest ships could moor, was the goat-pie man's shop, and of all the delicious smells that wafted around that part of the city, the smell coming from his spotless bakery was the deliciousest. The goat-pie man's goat pies were the finest in Meandermart – indeed, the finest in all of Rillia. Mutt could see them, neatly arranged on wooden shelves in the window, steaming up the glass with their delectable meaty aroma. As well as being the finest pies in the kingdom, they were also the most expensive, which was the reason Mutt had never tried one. He could see the goat-pie man standing in the doorway, his striped apron neatly ironed and his bald head catching the morning sunlight as he bellowed out over the heads of the passing crowd: 'Finest goat pies in all of Rillia! Simmered with a blend of eleven secret herbs and spices! Enjoyed by the crowned heads of all three of the Three Kingdoms! Only for the discerning! Only for the very best!' He caught sight of Mutt loitering on the corner and added, out of the corner of his mouth, 'Certainly not for the likes of you, street dog! Get out of it!' He reached behind him for a broom, but by the time he turned round again Mutt had vanished. 'Watch your pockets, lords and ladies!' yelled the goat-pie man. 'There's a street mutt in the neighbourhood! A nasty little pie-dog!' Round the corner, Mutt frowned. It was the goat-pie man who had given him his nickname in the first place, and he never seemed to tire of warning people about the boy he called a 'street mutt', implying he was some kind of thief or pickpocket. Mutt had never stolen anything in his life, even though he had nothing. 'We do not steal,' his father had always told him, and 'We do not beg,' his mother would always add. *Not that it had done them much good*, Mutt thought to himself glumly as another waft of fragrant goat-scented steam made his empty stomach wince.

I do not beg, Mutt repeated to himself as he carried on squeezing through the crowd, *and I do not steal*. So what did this lonely, barefoot boy do for food? The answer lay by the wharves, where the sides of the great riverboats rose up from the docks like wooden walls, strewn with ropes as their cargoes were loaded and unloaded. Here, there were always things to carry, things to be delivered. And, if you were fast, like Mutt, and you knew the city inside out, like Mutt, you could earn a few small copper coins for helping with that carrying and delivering. And so, by spending his day sprinting from one end of Meandermart to the other, clutching a letter or a parcel in his hands, Mutt was able to earn enough to buy himself something to eat for his supper. Not enough to buy a pie from the goat-pie man, which was far, far too expensive. Not enough to buy shoes either. But most days he scraped together just enough for a bowl of watery stew or a stale half-loaf from one of the smaller, shabbier shops that could be found towards the edge of the market.

On this particular Tuesday, Mutt returned to the Merchants' Quarter towards the end of the afternoon, looking for one last delivery before he went home. He wandered along the wharves, idly kicking his toes in the dirt as he gazed up at the busy sailors on their boats. 'Ah, there he is!' A voice broke into his reverie. 'That's the boy, the fast one. Hey! Come here!' A plump man in richly embroidered robes was beckoning to him from a booth on the other side of the street. 'I need this taking to the Mages' Quarter as quickly as possible,' the man said dismissively, holding out a thick piece of folded parchment between two of his sausage-like fingers. 'You know the way?'

Mutt nodded, but slightly reluctantly. Of course he knew the way to the Mages' Quarter – he knew the way to everywhere. But it meant going past the Knights' Academy, and classes would just be finishing for the day. The rich kids from the Academy never missed an opportunity to chase him if they saw him running past, and, although they didn't always catch him, it meant a beating and a ducking in the water trough if they did. Mutt silently weighed up the risks against the two tarnished coins the merchant was holding out along with his letter. After a few seconds he nodded again, more decisively. Snatching the letter along with his payment, he took off back through the market.

The Mages' Quarter was in the north-west of Meandermart, right on the other side of the city from the bustling wharves. Mutt knew it would take a good hour for him to weave his way there, even with the shortcuts he knew through the winding jitties and gannicks. He took the first forty minutes or so at a brisk pace, the looming shape of the castle showing itself between the buildings on his right from time to time. But, when he got close to the Knights' Academy, he slowed his pace, walking casually by on the other side of the street, desperate to avoid attracting attention to himself. Here and there he could see the red tunics of the trainee knights as they swaggered along in groups or pairs, their arms draped round one another's shoulders and their loud, confident voices ringing up and down the street. Mutt kept his head down, clutching the letter tightly and trying to hurry as fast as possible without breaking into a run, which would be sure to get him spotted.

It might sound rather glamorous and exciting, the Knights' Academy. But, in fact, the Knights of Rillia rarely did anything particularly useful. The golden, chivalrous days of fighting and rescuing were in the past, and the average knight was now more interested in keeping his or her armour shiny, and hanging around saying useless things like 'prithee' while waving a handkerchief. It was basically a handy career for people with very full purses and rather empty heads – somewhere for the rich merchant families to send their children if they didn't show much aptitude for anything in the merchanting line. As such, you won't be surprised to learn that the Academy was not exactly full of Rillia's finest brains. On the other hand, though, as its high towers and gleaming white walls would suggest, it was financed by some of Rillia's fattest wallets.

'Street mutt!' The braying voice made every hair on Mutt's body stand on end. He glanced over his shoulder to see a gaggle of Academy students pushing their way across the street towards him. Immediately, he broke into a frantic sprint and heard the braying cries of excitement as the kids in red tunics gave chase – **'There he goes!'**

'Looks like he needs a bath!'

'Get him!'

Through the winding streets Mutt ran, away from the Academy and into the Mages' Quarter, where the buildings were taller and more rickety, their street-facing walls leaning drunkenly out so that they seemed to close in above him like a tunnel. Left and right he weaved, the sounds of pursuit ringing in his ears, his bare feet slapping on the cold, damp ground. He dimly registered that he was about to pass the house to which he'd promised to deliver the letter and remembered the two coins he'd been paid. *I do not steal*, he reminded himself sternly, and wasted three valuable seconds tearing the door open and yelling 'Delivery!' before flinging the letter at the astonished-looking mage behind the counter. When Mutt tore off down the street again, the mage peered curiously after him from his door. He ducked quickly back inside as the gaggle of trainee knights thundered past, then leaned out again, twiddling his thin beard thoughtfully, following Mutt's fleeing form as it ducked round a corner and into the narrow, winding gannicks that made up most of the Mages' Quarter.

Which brings us, more or less, to the point where this chapter started. Because, after flinging himself round a few more corners – left, left, right, right, right, left – Mutt realized something rather alarming. For the first time ever in all his years of criss-crossing the enormous city of Meandermart, he had absolutely no idea where he was.

Mutt was lost, Mutt was hungry, Mutt was alone.

With the hunters from the Knights' Academy in hot pursuit, Mutt did the only thing he knew how to do really well. He just kept on running, knotting himself deeper and deeper into the winding ways of the Mages' Quarter, scanning frantically for familiar landmarks and clinging on to the hope that before long he'd realize where he was and work out a way to throw off his pursuers. But it didn't happen. No familiar landmarks presented themselves. The buildings were too tall and tightly packed for him to catch even a glimpse of the distant castle and work out which direction he was headed in. Mutt was lost.

Presently he ran at top speed into a small, deserted square. The few rapid corners he'd managed to throw in had gained him a bit of distance, but he could hear the clumping of feet not too far behind. Mutt's panicked eyes scanned the square for other exits and became even more panicked when he completely and utterly failed to find any. He dug his heels into the ground in a desperate attempt to stop himself, but his left foot hit a hidden stone and he found himself tumbling head over heels, getting coated in mud as he rolled across the square, before finally coming to a halt against a ramshackle wooden building that occupied the far side of it.

Throughout his fall, Mutt had been frowning in puzzlement. The building was strange for a number of reasons. Firstly, he had never seen it before – and he'd thought, up till now, he had seen every single building in Meandermart. Secondly, the building had a very odd, unfamiliar series of words written in neat black lettering above the door.

MAGICAL DETECTIVE AGENCY

Mutt didn't have issues with the first or the third word. 'Agency' – that was clear enough. And this was the Mages' Quarter, so it was not unusual for shops here to claim they were 'magical' in some way (even though, with so little magic left in the world, the word was usually being used to cover up some cheap sleight-of-hand trick or coloured powder). No, it was the middle word that was causing him a problem – that word 'detective'. It was a word Mutt had never heard before, for the simple reason that practically nobody had ever heard it before. It had, in fact, only been invented the previous month.

From his vantage point, lying flat on his back on the ground, Mutt squinted up at it, trying to work out what it could possibly mean. He was familiar with the word 'defective'; he knew that meant something that didn't work properly. But why on earth would someone write that above their door? Was it some kind of badly named repair shop? As he lay there, Mutt became aware of something else. Closer to him, on the wall to one side of the door, was a wooden sign with more writing on it. Wriggling backwards slightly on his shoulders, he managed to read:

**Conundrums untangled.
Mysteries demystified.
Riddles resolved.**

And just beneath that, someone had painted in different, slightly more untidy writing:

NO LOST CATS

None of this seemed to make things any clearer. But there was something else, too – more letters, picked out in the strangest of places. They were written along the bottom edge of the wooden sign, so nobody would ever see them unless they were, like Mutt, lying on the floor right in front of the building. He lifted himself up on his elbows to peer more closely at the neat letters written in that strange, inaccessible place.

Apprentice needed. Apply within.
Must look in unusual places.

This message was so strange and unexpected that it needed pondering. But pondering is a luxury only granted to those who aren't being chased. Mutt scrambled to his feet as the thundering of boots grew louder. And, as the trainee knights burst into the square after him, he wrenched open the door with that baffling word

DETECTIVE

written above it and plunged through, slamming it shut behind him.

CHAPTER 2

THE ACCIDENTAL APPRENTICE

Mutt turned, pressing his back against the door and wiping his sweaty hair out of his face. Behind him, he could hear a hubbub of conversation as the bullies discussed whether to follow him inside or not. He looked about him. He was standing on a rough doormat at one end of a large, well-swept room. Opposite him was a large fireplace with a sturdy wooden chest on the floor beside it and two tall wooden doors, one on each side. To his right, beneath a high window, was a neat and tidy desk.

The room appeared completely deserted. 'Hello?' said Mutt uncertainly.

At this point, something else extremely unexpected happened.

With a clonking noise, the wooden chest rose up on its four stubby legs and took a few steps towards him, tilting sideways slightly, looking for all the world like a curious dog. Mutt would have jumped back in shock if he hadn't already been pressed up against the door.

'Er . . . hello . . . boy?' he said to the chest uncertainly. In reply, it gave a skittish little leap and turned round quickly, emitting a strange creaking noise not unlike a bark. 'That's it,' said Mutt encouragingly. 'Good . . . wooden chest. Hello.' He walked a few paces forward across the floor, holding out his hand ahead of him.

At that moment, as if Tuesday hadn't turned weird enough already, the door on the left-hand side of the fireplace burst open to reveal a gigantic, shaggy figure framed in the opening. Mutt skittered backwards, bare feet squeaking on the wooden floor, and slammed himself back against the door. The shape moved forward into the room, the light from the window falling on the long, white fur that covered its body and reflecting in a pair of blazing yellow eyes that looked completely furious.

'**FEET!**' bellowed the creature as it advanced across the room towards Mutt.

'Erm,' said Mutt unhelpfully. 'Sorry, what?' he added.

'**FEET!**' the hulking monster repeated, reaching out with a stubby, clawed finger to point at the floor. Mutt looked down to see that his filthy feet had left a trail of mucky footprints. '**WIPE YOUR FEET!**' the hairy beast clarified.

'Ahm, ahm, I'm sorry,' gibbered Mutt, frantically scuffing his feet across the doormat. As he did so, there was a knock on the door.

'Send out the street mutt,' came a posh, braying voice from outside. 'He needs a bath. And a good thrashing into the bargain.'

The shaggy white-furred creature narrowed its yellow eyes. 'Who's that?' it asked Mutt suspiciously.

'Oh, them?' Mutt paused in his foot-wiping to point back over his shoulder with a thumb. 'They're always chasing me.'

'Oh, they are, are they?' The monster glared at the closed door, which the students of the Knights' Academy unfortunately chose that exact moment to fling arrogantly open, having grown bored of waiting for their quarry to emerge.

'Come on then, street dog,' said a girl in a richly lined green cloak, leading the rest of the trainee knights inside. She grasped Mutt firmly by the upper arm. (It's worth pointing out here that not a single one of them wiped their feet on the way in, which explains what happened next.)

The huge creature's white fur actually shook slightly with anger as it regarded the gaggle of muddy boots that had now congregated on the hitherto spotless floor. The Academy students stood dumbly, not having expected to encounter such a fearsome beast in this small, out-of-the-way shop. There was a wet plop as a large clump of mud detached itself from one of their boots and fell to the floor, joining the brown puddle already pooling there.

With three swift steps, the giant figure reached the girl in the green cloak and seized her firmly by the front of her tunic. 'WHY,' it roared, as her legs bicycled frantically beneath her, 'does nobody WIPE. THEIR. FEET? Look at THIS MESS!' The rest of the knights obediently looked down at the floor. This was a tactical mistake because, after catching hold of Mutt and pulling him free, the white-furred beast lobbed the green-cloaked girl at her friends like a bowling ball, sending them all skittling back outside, where they toppled over on to their backs in the mud. 'Now GET LOST!' it bellowed so loudly that the blast actually blew back the hair of the foremost few. Pushing and jostling each other in their hurry to be first to escape, the red tunics struggled to their feet, turned tail and fled from the square in terror.

'Thanks for that,' said Mutt as the gigantic creature stepped back into the room and closed the door. Mutt took a few nervous steps backwards, coming to rest against the desk. 'Sorry about the, you know, the floor,' he added, pointing to his dirty footprints.

'Yes, well,' the beast replied in a slightly calmer tone, 'I like to keep the place tidy.' It stumped over to the fireplace, where a mop and bucket were propped against the hearth. 'This stuff's flipping murder to clean,' it explained, stroking its long, pure white fur. It picked up the mop and bucket, carried them towards the door and began slopping soapy water over the muddied floor.

Mutt watched this process nervously. The white-furred creature was fully twice his height and probably three times his width. Thick muscles rippled beneath its pelt as it busily cleaned the floor. It was, Mutt knew, a snow gnoblin from the mountains to the far south of the Three Kingdoms. They were occasionally seen in the city streets, wading through the crowd, head and shoulders above all the other creatures. But Mutt had never seen one this large or this imposing before. Or indeed this obsessed with keeping its fur clean.

A TRAVELLER'S GUIDE TO RILLIA

SNOW GNOBLINS are a species unknown in my home country ~ where the only gnoblins are the common mountain variety ~ distinguished by their unusual size, horned heads and yellow eyes. The snow gnoblins of the mountains and tundra are a fierce and warlike race, distrustful of outsiders and mainly concerned with the unending wars between the different clans and their complicated hunting rituals.

They rarely venture outside their own lands, but they are occasionally glimpsed trading in the market cities of Rillia, exchanging gemstones mined in their mountain home for weaponry or fur~cleaning products.

'I keep telling him to shave it off,' came a new voice from directly behind Mutt.

With a strangled **'Flaargh!'** Mutt lurched forward as if something red hot had been pressed into his back, promptly slipped on a patch of mopped floor and fell over. Nobody had been behind him a moment ago, he was sure of it. But, when he craned his neck round, he could see that a girl about his own age was now sitting calmly in a chair with her feet propped up casually on the wooden desk. He lurched inelegantly to his feet, skidding in the soapy water like a roller-skating fawn. The girl watched this process with an expression of disapproval. She was, he could now see, dressed from toe to head in black leather, from the high boots encasing her feet and legs to the bandanna tied round her forehead. Above this, a complicated bun of braided hair was stuck through with objects that looked, at first sight, like the handles of several daggers. Which is because that's exactly what they were.

'Shave off my hair?!' thundered the snow gnoblin, outraged, as he continued mopping. 'And look like those bald northern gnoblins?'

'Well, Mirko, you're always complaining when it

gets dirty,' the girl told him, pulling a dagger out of her hair and balancing it, point down, on the tip of a finger. 'Be easier just to get rid of it, wouldn't it?'

'That is one of the most offensive things you have ever said, Nissassa,' Mirko replied, plunging his mop back into the bucket. 'And,' he added after a moment's thought, 'you have said several extremely offensive things to me today alone.'

The girl in black gave a mocking inclination of the head. 'Let's ask this grubby little boy, shall we?' she mused, leaning forward and gesturing at Mutt with the dagger. 'What do you think, boy? Should Mirko cut all his silly hair off?'

Mutt gaped at her. He wasn't sure which of this pair terrified him more: the gigantic gnoblin or the girl who seemed to be heavily armed both with weapons and sarcasm. A few faint squeaking sounds escaped his mouth as he struggled for a reply that wouldn't offend either of them.

'Well, that's very helpful, thanks,' the girl replied with a vague smile, tossing the dagger high into the air and catching it deftly in her bun without looking up.

'Do you have a mystery for me?' said another new

voice – a low, musical voice – from right behind Mutt, who once again leaped in shock and slipped over on the wet floor. Again he felt the chilly water soaking into his thin trousers. He was beginning to wish that the people who lived in this mysterious shop would announce their presence with a slight cough or something, rather than constantly startling him by saying enigmatic things unexpectedly in his ear. He paddled with his hands to turn himself round to see who had spoken this time. After the snow gnoblin and the leather-clad girl, he was prepared for almost anything.

Standing behind him, hands on hips, was a tall woman in a long blue cloak. Her long, white-blonde hair hung down on either side of her face like twin waterfalls, and her eyes glittered with interest as she looked at him.

'Do you have a mystery?' she repeated, as Mutt once again found himself incapable of speech. 'Why do you need a detective?' she asked more slowly.

'I don't actually know what that is,' Mutt admitted, struggling to his feet for the third time that day.

'The electink's gone wrong, I keep telling you,' said Nissassa from behind the desk. 'First there was that woman going on about her cat; now we've got random grubby kids wandering in off the street.' Mutt self-consciously tried to smooth down his tunic, which was, he had to admit, not especially clean.

'Give him a chance,' said the tall woman in a soothing tone.

'I saw your sign,' said Mutt abruptly, rather stung by Nissassa's attitude. She was treating him like an unwanted stray – and had described him as a 'kid', when they were clearly the same age.

'Yes,' the tall woman replied patiently. 'The sign on the door, for the Magical Detective Agency. I'm Clarity Jones, M.I.'

'Magical Investigator,' Nissassa added from behind him.

'I don't actually know what a . . . a detective is,' admitted Mutt. He heard Nissassa emit a small, scornful snort. 'But that's not the sign I meant,' he went on. 'I meant, I saw your notice advertising for an apprentice.'

In the sudden silence that followed, he realized that Mirko the snow gnoblin had stopped his mopping.

Clarity Jones looked at him appraisingly. 'Ah, you

saw my advertisement, did you?' she asked. 'You know how to look in unusual places?' There was a thudding sound as the wooden chest gambolled over to stand beside her, and she rubbed a hand absent-mindedly over its lid.

'He was being chased, Clarity,' said the snow gnoblin, coming to stand beside her too. 'Those wastrels from the Knights' Academy.'

Mutt nodded to confirm this. 'I fell down,' he admitted. 'I'm not sure I was really looking in an unusual place. Not in the way you're thinking perhaps.'

'Aha! Honest too,' said the woman approvingly. 'What's your name, boy-who-falls-over-a-lot?'

'They call me Mutt,' replied Mutt, blushing slightly. 'Well, the goat-pie man calls me Mutt. Nobody else calls me anything much. Not usually, my lady.' All three of the other people in the room laughed at this.

'I'm no great lady,' the woman reassured him, exchanging a glance with Mirko. 'Just Clarity will do. Clarity Jones, at your service . . . Mutt.' She gave him a slight bow.

'The greatest detective in Meandermart,' added

the snow gnoblin, looking at Clarity proudly.

'The *only* detective in Meandermart,' corrected the girl in black.

'And what is a detective, exactly, anyway?' Mutt couldn't help asking.

'Ah,' said the woman, holding up a finger. 'I'm glad you asked.'

'Everybody asks,' added the snow gnoblin.

'Thank you, Mirko,' the detective (whatever that might be) replied. 'Yes, it is something fairly new. Something I recently invented, in fact. Let me ask you a question, Mutt.' She placed a hand on his shoulder. 'What happens when something occurs that nobody can explain? A mysterious disappearance, say. Or a baffling murder.'

Mutt thought about this for a moment. Murders and disappearances were not that uncommon in the city of Meandermart. In a land where many people carried a sword and there was no police, maybe it wasn't incredibly surprising. Also, the city actually had an entire area known as the Assassins' Quarter. *So*, he thought, *what does happen when somebody vanishes, or gets knifed or poisoned in a tavern . . .?*

Mutt gave the most honest answer he could.

'Nothing happens,' he replied.

'Ex-*actly*.' Clarity Jones beamed at him. 'Nothing happens. Until now, that is. Because I've decided to become the city's first person who tries to work out who the culprit was. I'll *detect* them . . . see? A detective!'

'I still think "detector" would have been clearer,' grumbled the girl at the desk.

'Nobody even considered my suggestion,' added the big shaggy-furred gnoblin. 'Worker-outerer.'

'There wasn't room to write that above the door,' the detective told him. 'Now, Mutt,' she went on, 'you look like the kind of boy who might want to earn a few coins. Is that true?' Mutt nodded immediately, thinking of the pitiful wages he'd managed to earn that day delivering parchments around the city.

'But he only saw the sign by accident!' Nissassa pulled another dagger out of her hair and slammed the point into the desk, where it stuck, quivering, with an ominous *pa-doing*. 'He's not someone who normally looks in unusual places. He's just a kid who fell over!'

'Remember the electink, Nissassa,' said the

detective gently. 'Nobody is supposed to be able to find their way to those signs outside unless they need to be here.'

Nissassa gave another snort. 'And as I said,' she replied, 'it's obviously not working, is it? First cat woman, who keeps turning up even after we changed the sign, and now this useless boy! I don't even like cats.' She gave a small shiver. 'If I had a cat that went missing, I'd be calling a party planner, not a detective.'

As if on cue, there was a tremulous knocking at the door and a quavering voice cried out, 'Won't you please help me find Tiddles? He's been gone ever so long now. He'll be getting up to all kinds of mischief.'

The detective held a finger to her lips.

'I know you're in there,' the voice outside continued. 'I can see that big gnoblin through the window.' A wrinkled face appeared at the glass, framed by a halo of fuzzy white hair.

The snow gnoblin marched over to the window. 'For the last time,' he said firmly, 'this is the headquarters of the greatest detective –'

'The *only* detective,' interrupted Nissassa quietly.

'The *greatest* detective,' insisted the gnoblin, 'in all of Meandermart. She is waiting for exciting and unusual cases, OK? She is not available to help you find Tiddles.'

'We even changed the sign,' Nissassa added.

'Yes, I saw you changed the sign,' said the old lady querulously, 'but –'

'GO AWAY!' chorused the gnoblin and Nissassa. And, with a disappointed tut, the old lady's face vanished from the window.

'There you go,' Nissassa told the detective. 'All the proof you need that the magic on that electink has stopped working. Silly old woman looking for a lost cat,' she said, pointing to the door. Then, pointing at Mutt, 'And a boy who just got chased here, fell over and saw your advertisement by pure accident.'

Clarity Jones pondered this for a moment, a slight smile flickering on her face. 'Perhaps,' she said casually. 'But there's no harm in giving him a trial, is there? What do you say?'

'No,' replied Nissassa immediately, at exactly the same time as Mutt said, 'Yes, please!' He'd never been as confused as he had been in the last ten minutes, but he was also intrigued by this mysterious woman who called herself a Magical Investigator. Mutt had always been fascinated by the idea of magic, but had never expected to see any in real life. And the walking wooden chest was proof enough that something more than a little magical was going on in this odd, hidden-away shop deep in the Mages' Quarter.

'What kind of a trial?' asked Mirko, looking down at Mutt doubtfully. 'I can't see what use he's going to be.'

'My point exactly!' agreed Nissassa.

'Well, that's exactly what a trial is for, isn't it?' Clarity Jones said reasonably. 'What do you say, Mutt – if you help out for two weeks, and if you prove that you really can look in unexpected places, you get the job as Apprentice Detective. Deal?'

'Deal!' Mutt's eyes shone with excitement.

'He doesn't even have boots,' said Nissassa disapprovingly.

'Ah yes,' replied Clarity. 'Give our temporary assistant some money, will you, Nissassa? For incidental expenses. Like boots.' Then she turned and added to Mutt in a whisper. 'Get some boots.'

'And make sure you wipe them when you come in,' added Mirko sternly, but with what might have been a slight grin at the same time. It was difficult to tell behind the shaggy white fur.

There was a jingling as Nissassa rummaged inside the desk and pulled out a small, plump pouch.

'Here, temporary assistant,' she said, narrowing her eyes suspiciously. 'Catch.'

Mutt held up a hand as Nissassa threw the pouch to him and widened his eyes as it hit his palm with a heavy *thunk*. There was obviously more money inside than he'd ever held in his life.

'You can start in the morning,' suggested Clarity Jones, as Mutt stood looking dumbly at the pouch still clasped in his upraised hand. 'See you then, then.' She gave a nod of dismissal and Mutt, stuttering his thanks, backed out of the door, giving his bare feet an extra wipe on the mat as he did so.

'Of all the ridiculous things you've done,' said Nissassa drily when the door had closed again, 'that is by far the ridiculousest.'

'We shall see,' replied the detective calmly, as the wooden chest stood up on its hind legs, making a faint panting noise.

Mutt wasn't wasting any time. The afternoon sky was already beginning to darken and, for the first time in he didn't know how long, he had somewhere important to be. Dodging the frozen puddles, he raced back through the chilly streets of the Mages' Quarter, somehow now able to find his way much more easily. As he sprinted away, he barely even noticed the old woman who was still standing in the dusty little square and wailing, 'Please tell them to look for Tiddles!' The crowds that had filled the daytime streets were thinning now, and Mutt quickened his pace as he raced back towards the river. Skidding round the last corner so fast that he almost fell over again, he reached the goat-pie man's shop just as the owner was about to switch the sign on the door from OPEN to CLOSED.

'I've told you before,' said the goat-pie man pompously, seeing Mutt begin to climb the steps, 'I don't give out free pies. Not even at closing time. **Scram, street mutt!'**

'I don't want a free pie,' panted Mutt, pulling the pouch of coins from his tunic. 'I want to buy one.'

The goat-pie man was so taken aback that he dropped his CLOSED sign. It fell on to the top step with a clatter. 'You want to *what?*' he said faintly, leaning back against a doorpost.

'I want,' repeated Mutt with more confidence, 'to *buy* one goat pie, if you please. The finest one you have.'

Precisely forty-seven seconds later, Mutt was walking back down the steps. His pouch was lighter by a full twelve precious copper coins, but he felt as if his height had increased by around twelve feet, which he considered to be a very fair bargain. He could feel the warmth of the fresh pie clasped against his chest as he wound his way back down gannicks and jitties towards the east gate of the city and slipped out among the last of the day's travellers. Golden light began to touch the treetops as he left the road and ventured to the right, back towards the wide river, picking his way across the marshy area that Meandermartins called Squelj. The ground was swampy and dotted with tussocks of tall, spiky grasses, but the sure-footed Mutt dodged round these as he worked his way towards a large patch of woodland that lay beside a large bend in the river. Once he was among the trees, he slowed his pace, picking his way down a narrow track.

Right beside the river, hidden away among a stand of trees, tall and bent and with long, golden leaves that streamed down to touch the river below, stood a rickety wooden house. With its curved roof made of polished planks, it looked very much like an upturned boat, for the excellent reason that it *was* an upturned boat, washed up long ago and dragged to the top of this steep, rocky bank. Beneath the boat, clever hands had dug deep into the clay, fashioning strong walls with round windows that looked out across the brown waters of the River Rill. Mutt, taking an automatic glance back over his shoulder, pushed his way through the door and down a few steps.

'**Mum, Dad – I'm home!**' he called as he entered the neat, compact room. It was warm and dimly lit inside, the evening light filtering through the long leaves outside and further softened by the thick greenish glass of the windows. 'Weird day today,' he continued. 'I got chased by the Knights' Academy kids again and ended up in a part of the Mages' Quarter I'd never seen before. And then, you'll never guess what . . . I got offered a job! Well, a trial anyway. I'm working for this lady who's a detective. You know what that is? No, neither did I until an hour ago . . .'

Mutt kept chatting as he moved across the room towards a wooden hatch set in the opposite wall. 'There's this really scary girl there with knives in her hair, and a big snow gnoblin. And this magical chest! It's actually the best thing that's happened for ages.' As he spoke, the fading light fell on two squat wooden figures that looked out across the room from a high shelf. They were lifna, those wooden effigies used by Rillians to remember relatives who had died. And these particular lifna represented Mutt's parents.

'She even gave me some money right away,' Mutt went on, tugging at the hatch in the wall. It led out on to a small ledge set right out over the river. 'I know!' Mutt continued, smiling up at the figures. 'Amazing, isn't it? Look what I bought!' He pulled out the goat pie, waving it proudly in the air to show the statues before climbing out on to the ledge. There he sat, legs dangling over the water as the long leaves swayed and rustled on either side.

Mutt's mother and father had always proudly told him, 'We do not steal,' and, 'We do not beg.' And neither of them ever had, despite being so poor that most of us would have understood if they *had* done both. But they had been so poor and so hungry that they hadn't been able to fight off the disease that had raged through the kingdoms three years ago. And so the wooden lifna were all that remained for Mutt to tell about his day.

Out on the ledge, a cloud of savoury steam puffed into Mutt's face as he broke the pie crust, and through the meat-scented mist he saw one of the ships that had been moored at the wharf earlier slipping past, beginning its two-day journey to the Great Sea, unimaginably far away to the east. Mutt knew that, somewhere out there, three great rivers met. He knew that beyond that point, on the coast, were the Twin Cities, where great towers and castles faced each other across a wide bay. He'd heard merchants swapping tales down at the wharves as he waited for work, never dreaming of the remotest chance he'd ever see the Twin Cities for himself. And he knew that further away still, out in the open ocean, was the high rocky island where the golden Citadel of the Overqueen stood in solitary splendour.

As the ship passed him, speeding up as it steered into the faster currents towards the centre of the river, one of the sailors at the rail spotted Mutt sitting with his pie among the tall trees. She waved her hand in salute, and he returned the gesture, holding his pie aloft in an entirely appropriate gesture of triumph. And then, finally, as the ship disappeared beyond the trees, he lowered the pie and took his very first bite.

And so, as the evening tree shadows spread their long fingers out along the river, reaching towards the unknown west, Mutt ate the best goat pie he had ever tasted – the *only* goat pie he had ever tasted – while the wooden effigies of his mother and father watched in silent approval from the darkening boat-house behind him.

CHAPTER 3

THE PERPLEXING PUZZLE OF THE FLYING FOOL

Sometime deep in the night it began to rain – the cold rain you get in the very dead of winter that's only a smidge away from turning to snow. It trickled and hissed through the trees beside the river, hitting the sluggish stream outside the boat-house like icy needles. Inside, though, beneath the thick planks of the boat-roof and dug deep into the soil of the riverbank, the room was warm and peaceful. Mutt, wrapped in a threadbare blanket, half woke to the comfortable sound of the downpour on the wooden hull above him. His sleepy ears caught the plip and hiss of drops running from the roof into the river below. But, just as he was about to drift back off into the best sleep – the sort of sleep you have while it rains outside on a cold night – he suddenly sat bolt upright. His ears had found some new sounds, somewhere out in the rain. Sounds that meant danger. The plashing of large feet on the narrow path that led to his house. The snap and whip of a branch being pushed to one side.

Someone was coming.

In a flash, Mutt rolled from his low wooden bed on to the floor and wriggled across the small room to peer out of the round, porthole-like window beside the door. His eyes struggled to pick anything out among the dark trees and the streams of rain. Dawn was still an hour or more away and the night was lit only by the unwholesome, monochrome moonlight. Squinting, he looked left and right and then froze. A huge shape was approaching, white and hulking in the gloom. There was a louder snapping and a muttered oath as the shape made its way down the slight slope to the front door, and with a startled gasp Mutt threw himself to the door and jerked it open. There, dripping wet, with his sopping white fur plastered to his skin, was Mirko, the enormous snow gnoblin.

'Mirko!' said Mutt in a half-whisper. In the night, it's hard not to half-whisper stuff, even when there's nobody else around. 'What are you doing here?'

'We've got a case,' Mirko replied, standing on one leg so he could wring out his right calf on the doormat. 'Clarity wants you.'

'How did you know where to find me?' asked Mutt, baffled. This was the first visitor he could ever remember coming to his door.

'Hmm, you're still not quite clear, are you, on what detectives do,' replied Mirko with a slight smile. He peered past Mutt, down the stairs into the gloom of the house. 'This where you live?' he asked, taking a couple of steps down. Mutt, nodding, stood to one side to let him pass. A gap somewhere in the clouds had allowed fingers of moonlight to bounce off the river and seep through the portholes, giving the room a faint silvery glow. 'Cosy,' said Mirko approvingly, looking around. 'And clean,' he added with even more enthusiasm. 'So, you live here with your parents?' he asked.

'Erm . . .' Mutt shuffled his feet on the stairs. But

before he could explain Mirko's yellow eyes had found the two wooden figures on the mantelpiece. Wordlessly, the huge snow gnoblin turned and placed an enormous hand on the boy's shoulder and held it there for a moment. It felt oddly comforting, despite also feeling as if a hugely heavy, sharp-taloned bird had landed on him, and Mutt gave a watery smile in reply.

'Come on,' said Mirko after a few moments. 'I'm already freezing, soaking wet and completely filthy. Let's not make it worse by being late as well.' Mutt saw that the gnoblin was indeed caked in mud from the waist down. Unlike Mutt, Mirko hadn't known the safest, cleanest way through Squelj and had evidently sunk in the deep mud several times on his way. Mutt tried to imagine for a moment what it must be like having to clean that long, white fur and decided he understood completely why Mirko had asked him so forcefully to wipe his feet the previous day. He followed the snow gnoblin back up the stairs and, locking the door carefully behind him, went with the hulking white shape back through the moonlit trees.

'There you are!'

Clarity Jones was standing in the doorway of the Magical Detective Agency as Mutt and Mirko raced into the square. The rain had finally stopped as they'd been running back through the city, and although Mirko's fur had started to dry out slightly, it still looked as if half of him had been dipped in dark chocolate like a posh biscuit.

'Give me a minute, give me a minute,' said Mirko peevishly, pushing past Clarity into the front room. 'I can't go out on a case looking like this, can I?' Mutt heard clanking sounds from inside the agency as the snow gnoblin grumbled on. 'Nobody told me the new kid lived on the other side of a stinking marsh, did they? What's wrong with living here in Meandermart like everybody else?'

'Property prices,' said Mutt with a shrug. 'My budget is precisely zero.'

Clarity gave him a friendly smile, standing aside slightly and ushering him inside. A fire was crackling in the large grate on the other side of the room, and in front of this stood Mirko, dipping a large wooden comb in a bucket of water and dragging it through his muddy fur.

'Doesn't that hurt?' asked Mutt curiously, moving closer. He dimly remembered his mother tugging knots out of his thick, dark hair when he was little and how it had felt.

'Of course it hurts,' replied the gnoblin moodily. 'But, if this dries, I'll never get it out.' He continued combing.

'I'm still available to shave it all off for you if you change your mind,' said a voice from away to the right. The girl, Nissassa, emerged from a side door, tucking a long, slim dagger down the back of her black leather jacket.

Clarity sighed. 'Another dagger? You won't be allowed to take any of them inside, you know.'

'You know my motto,' replied Nissassa, spreading her arms wide and suddenly producing two more knives, apparently from her sleeves. 'You can never have too many daggers.'

'Nissassa's an assassin,' Clarity explained to Mutt with a slightly weary look.

'Retired assassin,' the girl corrected, shrugging her shoulders and somehow making the knives disappear up her sleeves again. 'But it never hurts to be prepared. Unlike you, street dog –' she threw a sneer in Mutt's general direction – 'who doesn't even have boots on.'

Clarity looked down at Mutt's muddy, bare feet. 'You didn't buy boots?'

'Pie,' he explained, with an apologetic expression. Clarity Jones looked at him thoughtfully for a moment, then gave a brief nod of understanding. After all, there's nothing better to buy than a pie. Not when you really think about it. And certainly not when you've eaten nothing but watery stew and stale bread for three entire years.

'Come on, then,' ordered Clarity. 'Let's get on the case. **Here, Smyll!'**

The wooden chest came charging out of the door, turning excited circles and doing little leaps in anticipation of a walk.

'I'm not nearly clean yet!' complained Mirko, gesturing with his comb. He'd managed to shift a lot of the mud, but he still looked as if half of him was made of chocolate, albeit milk chocolate now rather than dark.

'You'll have to do as you are,' Clarity told him. 'Nissassa, are you ready?'

'I just need one more dagger,' the girl replied. She

was rummaging in one of the drawers of her desk beside the window.

Clarity tutted. 'How many daggers do you have with you already?' she asked sternly.

'One too few,' came the reply. 'Ah, here it is.' Nissassa pulled a squat throwing knife from the drawer and tucked it neatly behind her ear. 'Ready!'

'Come on then,' said Clarity Jones with a small sigh, and she led them out and locked the door firmly behind them.

'Where are we going, anyway?' Mutt asked Mirko as they followed Clarity and Nissassa through the scruffy, nondescript square and out into the winding ways of the Mages' Quarter.

'Castle,' the snow gnoblin replied with a sideways glance. Mutt's brain felt like it had just hiccupped.

'What castle?' he spluttered, not quite able to take it in. 'Not . . . not *the* castle? Not the big one?'

'How many castles do you know in Meandermart?' reasoned Mirko. Mutt racked his brains. He knew the streets inside out. *Surely there must be a shop or an inn called Ye Olde Castle or something*, he thought to himself. There was no way that he, Mutt, street runner from the age of eight, could be about to follow these mysterious new friends into the *actual* Meandermart Castle, the landmark high on the hill in the centre of the city. To him, it was more a navigational aid than a place where people might actually go.

'We've been summoned by the duchess,' said Clarity as she strode south towards the river, Smyll capering along at her heels. Mutt's brain did an even larger hiccup, or possibly a small brain burp. Duchess Peruka was the Warden of Meandermart and ruled over the entire city. Mutt had only ever caught sight of her once, when she'd been driven past him in a very elaborate carriage pulled by five gleaming white tricorns. He'd been granted a brief glimpse of some very high hair and a lot of jewellery before one of the castle guards running alongside the carriage (a squat man with bright red hair, Mutt remembered) had pushed him roughly back with a grunt and an 'Out of the way, street dog'.

A TRAVELLER'S GUIDE TO RILLIA

TRICORNS are a common beast of burden in Rillia. With their distinctive three horns atop their white heads, these proud animals run wild in the forests but are often tamed and used to pull carriages. They are also hunted for their skins, which are used to make hats.

In the wild, tricorns fight each other for supremacy over the other members of the herd. The winner is determined when it knocks off one of its opponents horns. A tricorn with one horn missing (also called a bicorn) is tolerated in the herd, but one that has lost two of its horns is banished. These outcast creatures ~ so-called monocorns ~ tend to wander off on their own, nobody knows where, and must look completely ridiculous.

Meandermart Castle sat on a high, rocky ridge right in the centre of the city. To the north, the castle was surrounded by steep cliffs and the calm, blue waters of the curved Oxbow Moat. To the south, the cliffs lowered slightly, and one wide, steep road led up to the main gates. It was the only way in or out, and Mutt had never dared climb it because of the huge amount of security.

You see, whichever duke or duchess controlled the city of Meandermart also controlled the main trading centre in all of Rillia. That meant they could collect tax every time anything was bought or sold and become enormously, hugely, cheek-puffingly rich. And that, in turn, led to all the other dukes and duchesses getting jealous and deciding that they'd quite like some of that money for themselves, thanks very much. And when they'd decided that, they quite often came to the conclusion that if the existing duke or duchess of Meandermart was to, say, take a tumble from the castle cliffs, or get stabbed or poisoned, then they could take their place. Taking all this into account, it's perhaps not too surprising to learn that the dukes and duchesses of Meandermart were (a) often fairly short-lived, and consequently (b) extremely jumpy, and therefore (c) fairly keen on staying in their nice safe castle and not admitting that many visitors. Which is a long-winded way of explaining that you didn't just amble up to the entrance of Meandermart Castle and knock on the door.

At the bottom of Castle Hill, two stout towers flanked the road that led steeply up towards the honey-coloured stone turrets and battlements far above. Both of the towers were heavily guarded and, as the members of the Magical Detective Agency approached, Mutt could see torchlight reflecting off the highly polished steel of weapons. Two hulking figures in armour barred their way, swords drawn.

'Who approaches?' barked one of the guards harshly.

'Clarity Jones, M.I.,' stated Clarity. 'That's Magical Investigator,' she explained. 'I'm a detective.'

'What's a petestive?' asked the guard scornfully. But Clarity Jones, who was already getting slightly tired of answering that question only a few weeks into her new career, ignored him.

'The duchess summoned us,' she told the guard, fixing him with a level, confident gaze, which is usually the best way to look at guards. 'It's urgent. She'll be *very* displeased if she finds out we've been delayed.'

Grumbling, the guard stumped off to the left-hand tower and, after a hurried conversation with somebody inside, came back. 'You may pass,' he said grudgingly. 'All weapons are to be left at the Strangers' Tower.'

Halfway up the hill was another pair of heavily fortified towers, standing even closer together than the lower ones. Here, they were led into a straw-floored room on the ground floor, where a stern-looking woman gestured towards a low wooden table and ordered them to leave all their weapons behind. Clarity Jones unbuckled a short sword from her belt and laid it carefully on the table, and Mirko pulled a stout wooden club from his belt. For Nissassa, however, it wasn't quite such a simple process.

'*All* my weapons?' she questioned as she approached the table.

'All of them,' the guard confirmed in a no-nonsense tone.

'I warned you,' said Clarity with a sigh.

Nissassa rolled her eyes. 'Very well,' she said grudgingly, and, while the guard watched, her eyes widening, the girl in black began to pull a bewildering variety of metalwork from a bewildering variety of places.

Mutt edged forward to get a better view; he'd heard stories about the secretive assassins of Meandermart, but he'd never seen one in the flesh before. If you ever saw one in the flesh, it usually meant your day was about to go downhill extremely fast. There was a clanking and a tinkling as Nissassa pulled several small, slim knives from the plaits in the top of her hair and piled them on the table. But that wasn't all. There was, as we know already, a throwing knife behind her ear. There were also, it turned out, slim swords tucked down each of her boots, throwing stars disguised as buttons on her leather jacket, and slim metal wires wrapped round each wrist that made Mutt wince just to look at – they gave the impression of being extremely deadly things to suddenly find wrapped round anything, your neck in particular, and he had a horrible suspicion that that was exactly what they were for. The pile on the table in front of Nissassa continued to grow, as the guard watched in complete disbelief. A long, flat sword was produced from the back of her neck and a pair of small, stout axes from her belt. Finally she twitched the two daggers out of her sleeves and stuck them firmly in the wooden tabletop. 'Take special care of those two,' she told the guard sternly. 'They're my favourites.' The guard nodded, her face pale and her mouth hanging open.

'Finished?' asked Clarity Jones drily from the doorway.

'I think so, yes,' replied Nissassa, frowning. 'Oh . . . no, not quite.' She clicked her fingers. 'I forgot Genevieve.' She reached her left hand up to her right shoulder, pulling yet another blade from a concealed sheath and plonking it on the table. 'Ready!' she told Clarity brightly.

'One of your daggers has a name?' asked Mutt in an undertone as they left the Strangers' Tower and continued up the steep causeway towards the gigantic wooden drawbridge.

'*All* my daggers have names, street dog,' she replied with a pitying expression. 'Just pray that I never have to introduce you to Francesca.'

With a clanking of enormous chains, the drawbridge began to descend. *First the goat pie*, thought Mutt as they walked through the archway, *and now this*. It really was turning into a rather extraordinary week.

The throne room of Meandermart Castle was extremely impressive. Well, it would be, wouldn't it? When you're designing a castle, you don't put the throne room in as an afterthought, do you? Its towering, vaulted ceilings stretched away from the main doors towards a high stained-glass window perched right on top of the cliffs, meaning the throne that sat in front of this window was framed by a truly magnificent backdrop. It included a panorama of the sprawling city and a view stretching across the farmlands of northern Rillia and further out towards the barren and treacherous Draconian Wastes far beyond. Basically, it was the best seat in the house. Thrones generally are.

At that time of the morning, the throne room would normally have been empty, but that day the castle was in uproar. And instead of still lying in her extremely big bed, the Duchess Peruka, Warden of Meandermart, was sitting on her throne, tapping her fingers impatiently.

The duchess was an impressive-looking person. And what was going on on top of her head was even more impressive. Recently the fashion among the richest people in Rillia had been to wear more and more elaborate wigs. This had led to what is best described as a wig arms race: a huge and extremely well-funded 'Who's got the biggest wig?' competition – a competition that, as Mistress of the Castle and Warden of Meandermart, the duchess simply *had* to win. To be out-wigged would be simply unthinkable. The wig she was now forcing herself to wear was so high that it needed a special servant to hold it upright by means of a richly carved wooden pole. The servant stood behind her, his arms shaking as he struggled to keep the wig more or less upright. The Magical Detective Agents approached the throne through a throng of sleepy, gossiping courtiers.

'Are you the detective?' asked Duchess Peruka in a ringing voice – the sort of voice that's used to being obeyed. (You don't fight your way to that kind of job without a very strong voice game.) As she spoke, she gestured with her hands and, when her sleeves rode up, Mutt noticed that her hands and wrists were covered in angry-looking red scratches.

'I wasn't sure you'd know what a detective was, Your Marvellousness,' replied Clarity Jones honestly.

The Warden of Meandermart examined Clarity keenly. People didn't usually speak back to her with such calm confidence. 'I know everything that happens in my city, madam,' she said in a tone that was fractionally less ringing. Clarity inclined her head graciously. 'I know your companions, or two of them at least: Nissassa, formerly of the White Hand Clan –' Nissassa dropped into a low bow – 'and the snow gnoblin from the Great Southern Mountains named Mirko.' Mirko waved a hairy arm in greeting. 'But him,' she said, pointing at Mutt, 'that barefoot boy, I can't place.' Mutt shuffled his feet awkwardly, reminding himself to buy those boots as soon as the markets opened. 'And I don't know where you originally come from, Clarity Jones,' the duchess continued, 'but you are gaining quite a reputation as a solver of mysteries.' Again, Clarity gave that delicate dip of her head without speaking. At the mention of the word 'mysteries', Smyll darted out from behind her cloak, panting excitedly.

'To business then,' declared the duchess, standing up suddenly and almost catching her wig-holder off guard. He had practically dozed off on his feet during the introductions, and as the duchess stood up he narrowly avoided jerking the entire wig from her head, which would have been, at the very least, a sacking offence. Quite possibly a banishing one, or even, considering the mood the duchess was in, an executing one. 'I have a mystery for you,' the duchess went on, sweeping majestically down the steps in front of her throne and taking Clarity by the arm. 'My jester has gone missing.'

'*Humph!* Sounds ideal,' grunted Nissassa, who found jesters incredibly irritating, and not without reason. Of all the occupations in this kind of castle setting, jestering is without doubt the most annoying. They're always capering about, ringing the tinkly bells on their hats and making bad jokes. But among the great and good of Rillia, like their ever-expanding wigs, having a jester was a massive status symbol and anybody who was anybody had a jester. In our world, the equivalent would probably be a yacht. But yachts rarely caper about and they don't wear hats with bells on, which means yachts are more useful than jesters and hardly ever call you 'nuncle'.

'I'm expecting some very important guests for the Moaningtide commiserations next week,' the duchess went on, leading Clarity back down the throne room,

Mutt and the others trailing behind. 'Some *very* important guests,' she repeated, nodding significantly, which was tough work for the wig-holder. 'And when they arrive, I simply must have Handy Dandy back. To welcome such illustrious company without a jester . . . well, you don't know how shameful that would be. How could you?' She looked rather patronizingly at Clarity and her companions. 'But, please believe me when I tell you that it's absolutely vital that you find out what's happened to him with all speed. I'm prepared to pay handsomely, of course – if you accept the task.' That last sentence might look as if it was a question, but it really wasn't. The Duchess of Meandermart didn't ask for help; she demanded it.

'Of course, Your Marvellousness,' replied Clarity Jones. 'I just have a few questions to start with, if that's permitted.'

While Clarity began to ask Duchess Peruka whether Handy Dandy the jester had ever gone missing before, and what his usual habits were, Mutt looked around the throne room. Servants and richly dressed rich people stood here and there, looking tired and nervous. And leaning against a stone pillar, not far away from him, was a young man with long, golden hair. He was watching the duchess with a slight smile on his handsome face, his legs crossed and his arms folded. Mutt recognized him immediately: it was Underduke Ferdinand, the duchess's younger brother. He was well known and well liked around Meandermart. Unlike his sister, he was fond of walking the streets, talking to ordinary people, and was famous for his generosity, often giving gifts to people who seemed to be in need. He had a particular interest in strange creatures and could often be found talking to the sailors along the wharf, asking them about the animals they had encountered on their travels and paying them well for any they had brought back.

Catching Mutt looking, the young man gave a wink and beckoned him over. 'Hello, hello,' he said kindly.

'Bit early in the morning for all this, isn't it?'

'Good morning, sir,' replied Mutt, smiling despite his nervousness. There was something about the underduke's friendly face that made you want to smile back at him.

'A missing jester, eh?' mused Ferdinand. 'How very intriguing. I wonder what's happened. Are you one of these . . . What did my sister call them? Detractors?'

'Detectives, sir,' Mutt corrected him politely.

'Come to find Handy Dandy?' Underduke Ferdinand stifled a yawn. 'Well, don't be in too much of a hurry. Between you and me, his jokes were more than a little irritating. He was always coming up behind me with an inflated pig's bladder and making ridiculous noises with it. Very trying. Put me right off my supper.' He winked again and Mutt grinned in return, glancing over his shoulder to make sure he wasn't required. Clarity and the others were clustered round the duchess, listening to her intently. When he turned back again, the young man leaning against the pillar was staring curiously at his feet. Mutt blushed, thinking he was about to be on the receiving end of another patronizing comment of the 'barefoot boy' variety. But instead the handsome man grinned.

'That looks very comfortable,' he said in a friendly tone. 'I don't know why more people don't go around without boots. In fact –' still leaning against the pillar, he lifted a leg and tugged off an expensive-looking brown boot – 'I think I might join you.' And, showing the thoughtfulness and generosity that made him so popular throughout the city, Underduke Ferdinand threw his boots down on the stone floor, where they landed with a thud of soft leather. 'Why don't you look after those for me?' he asked Mutt. 'They look about your size. Believe me, I've got far too many and I'm running out of cupboard space.'

Mutt began to gabble some words of thanks, but at that point he was interrupted by a cry from the duchess. **'Ferdinand!'** she barked officiously, and the young man uncoiled himself from his pillar-leaning position and wandered casually over towards his sister.

'Yes, Your Marvellousness?' he said with a bow.

'This is my younger brother, Underduke Ferdinand,' the duchess told Clarity. 'He will show you to Handy Dandy's chambers and provide you with any other assistance you may need. Let that be the penalty, Ferdinand, for presenting me with that awful animal,' she added with a disapproving look.

'I gave her a cat as a present,' the underduke explained to Mutt with an amused expression, 'but they didn't get on very well.' Mutt, remembering the scratches on the duchess's arms, nodded, and thought that perhaps he was very slightly on the cat's side here. 'Of course, sister,' said the underduke out loud with another, shallower bow. 'Come on,' he went on, giving Mutt a friendly and encouraging pat on the shoulder. 'This way, my friends,' he called to Clarity, Nissassa and Mirko, beckoning them to follow him as he strode out of the throne room with a slap of bare feet on the chilly stone. Mutt jogged along in their wake, clutching his new boots tightly to his chest.

Ten minutes later, the Duchess of Meandermart was safely back in bed, having been reassured that the city's finest – and only – detective team was on the case. Her wig-supporting servant was bathing his aching arms in ice-cold water from the moat, and Clarity Jones, Nissassa, Mirko and Mutt were being led up a steep spiral staircase inside one of the narrow towers that ringed the outer walls of the castle.

'This is where he lives,' said Underduke Ferdinand when they reached the top of the stairs. 'The annoying little twerp,' he added under his breath. (Even though it's part of being a noble to have a jester, nobody really likes them.) They found themselves in a small round room, with windows looking out over the city. One of these stood open. 'The duchess called for him very late last night, after the feast,' Ferdinand explained as Clarity began walking around examining things, Smyll the chest trotting alongside her. 'When he didn't appear, she sent me up here to find him. And when he wasn't here, we searched the whole castle,' he went on. 'Then, when nobody could find him, the duchess said, "Call for that detective!" And I said –'

'You said, "What's a detective?"' guessed Mirko, who'd had trouble squeezing himself up the narrow staircase.

'That's right,' said Underduke Ferdinand in surprise. 'How did you know?'

'It's what everyone says,' replied the snow gnoblin. 'What do you reckon, Clarity? Any clues?'

'It all looks pretty normal in here,' replied Clarity

Jones, who had moved over to a wooden bed beneath the open window. 'Well, someone's definitely been lying on this,' she said, poking the blanket with a long finger.

Mutt, meanwhile, after leaving his new boots tidily just inside the doorway, had picked up a small leather-bound book that was lying face down in the middle of the floor. He turned it over and read the cover.

'He's always got his nose stuck in that book,' said Ferdinand, coming over to join Mutt and reading over his shoulder.

Ye Jester's Companion

A Most Excellente Compendium of Divertinge Caperynges, Japes and Pranks

Mutt opened the book at random. *A moste risible piece of frivolitie*, he spelled out slowly, *is to take ye inflated bladder of ye pigge and stryke ye gentlefolk full roundly upon ye head.* 'I think I'm beginning to see why you're not too keen on this Handy Dandy being found,' he told the underduke.

'Not alive, at any rate,' added Nissassa with a brief, wolfish smile. Ferdinand glanced at her slightly nervously.

'**Smyll!**' Clarity Jones clicked her fingers and the wooden chest galloped to her side on its stumpy legs, flinging open its lid. 'Let's see what we can uncover, shall we?' said the detective to herself, looking around the bedchamber.

Mutt, fascinated, edged closer to peer inside the chest. It was tightly packed with boxes, bottles and strange devices. 'What is all this?' he asked Clarity softly.

'You'll find out when you're ready,' she told him. 'If you pass your trial period and get taken on as my apprentice, that is. I've collected all these over many, many years,' she went on, bending over the chest with an expression of concentration. 'They're very rare and very, very valuable. So don't touch.' Mutt had been reaching out a curious finger, fascinated by some of the labels he could see on the bottles and boxes.

Blue Print

he read on one. Another said:

Mismatch Catcher

'Is that magic?' he asked, pointing to a stout wooden club that nestled in a long compartment along one side.

'No,' Clarity told him curtly. 'Even with all the magic in the world, sometimes you just have to hit someone on the head.'

'She's right, you know,' confirmed Nissassa with another wolfish grin.

'I think we'll try the witness powder, please, Smyll,' declared Clarity Jones. And, with a brief bark from the wooden chest and a jingling clatter from its contents, a wooden box of orange powder rose up slightly and Clarity, taking a pinch, sprinkled some into the palm of her hand. 'Stand aside, please,' she told the others, moving to the doorway of the chamber. Pursing her lips, she blew the powder on to the wooden door, which was still standing open. With a creaking sound, the door came slowly to life.

'Good morning,' said the door. (Doors usually have excellent manners.)

'And the same to you,' replied Clarity Jones. 'Sorry to disturb you, but Handy Dandy has gone missing. I don't suppose you could tell us what happened last night, could you?'

'He came upstairs,' recalled the door, 'carrying the cat.'

'The cat you gave to your sister?' Mutt asked Ferdinand, and out of the corner of his eye he saw Clarity Jones look at him sharply.

'That's right,' said the underduke. 'The jester took a shine to the thing, and as it wouldn't stop scratching my sister he sort of adopted it.'

'Is my story of no interest to anyone?' complained the door petulantly.

'Our apologies,' said Clarity politely. 'So Handy Dandy came upstairs, bringing the cat with him . . .?'

'He came inside, yes,' agreed the door, 'and closed me. Then I heard the rustling of pages. He must have been reading that book. He's always reading it.'

'Couldn't you see what was happening inside the room?' asked Mirko.

'Absolutely not!' said the door, scandalized. 'I

would never look at what was happening inside the room! It goes against everything I believe in!'

Mutt thought about this for a moment and found that he was rather relieved.

'But you could see the staircase?' pressed Clarity. 'Who else came up here?'

'Well, nobody did,' said the door, sounding sleepy now. There wasn't long before the witness powder wore off.

'But who else opened you?' the detective wanted to know.

'Nobody did,' the door repeated. 'Nobody until the underduke came looking for Handy Dandy after –' it broke off to give a gigantic yawn before continuing – 'after the banquet. And he wasn't here. I was closed the whole time. Now I really must . . .' With a snore, the door lapsed into silence.

'So Handy Dandy comes up here,' said Nissassa thoughtfully, 'and nobody else opens the door, but later that same night the jester's completely vanished.' She tapped the stone walls with expert fingers. 'This tower's too narrow for any hidden passages,' she went on. 'There's no other way out except . . .' At the same time, all four members of the Magical Detective

Agency looked towards the arched window above the bed. They all ran towards it at the same time, but, with her assassin skills, Nissassa was fastest. Vaulting up on to the bed, she stuck her head and shoulders out of the large arched opening in the wall. The tower was on the very edge of the castle, and below the window the cliff dropped sharply to a rocky platform far below, on the edge of the Oxbow Moat.

'No sign of smooshed jester down there,' Nissassa told the others, sounding more than a little disappointed.

'So . . . he didn't leave by the door,' said Clarity Jones to herself, pacing the room with her eyes half closed in thought. 'And he didn't fall from the window. Let's see . . .' She clicked her fingers and the wooden chest skittered across the stone floor to join her by the bed. 'Time trumpet please, Smyll.' A wooden object that looked to Mutt like an ordinary drinking horn, but open at both ends, rose slowly up from inside the chest and the detective grasped it.

'This is all most fascinating,' said Underduke Ferdinand, leaning forward to get a closer look. 'And what might this strange device be, madam?'

'The time trumpet allows me to hear what happened in the past,' replied Clarity, turning a small wooden dial that was set into the instrument.

'Can we all hear?' asked Mutt excitedly.

'I'll put it on speaker,' agreed Clarity, adjusting the dial again. 'Right – complete silence, please! As with the witness powder, we only get one shot at this, so listen closely.' She carefully laid the time trumpet on the bed and stepped back. Mutt strained his ears . . . There seemed to be a faint sound coming from the larger end of the horn. It sounded not unlike the rain on the roof of his boat-house the previous night: a deep thrumming noise.

'It's the cat!' whispered Mirko. 'Handy Dandy was in here with the cat! It's purring!' Clarity silenced him with an upraised finger, cupping her other hand behind her ear. Mutt picked out another noise above the cat – a tiny rustling of paper. In his mind's eye he could see Handy Dandy sitting on the bed, a contented cat upon his lap, flicking through his joke book.

Nissassa began to speak. 'It doesn't sound like there's any–' she began, but stopped abruptly as new, strange noises began to emerge from the time trumpet. There was a tearing, squelching sound, then a short, terrified exclamation. Then both of these were drowned out by a scuffling, scraping, ripping sound that rapidly faded into silence. No purring cat; no flicking pages. The members of the Magical Detective Agency exchanged glances.

'What was that?' asked Underduke Ferdinand. 'What happened?'

'I don't know,' replied Clarity, her eyes glittering with the excitement that only an unsolved puzzle could bring. 'But I'm going to find out.'

'But where did he go?' Ferdinand went on. 'Not out through the door, and not through the window, unless . . .' He gave a short laugh. 'I mean –' He kicked with a bare foot at the bedclothes, as if Handy Dandy would suddenly pop out and reveal he was just really, really good at hiding. 'I mean,' he repeated, 'jesters can't *fly*. The whole thing's completely impossible.'

Clarity Jones raised her eyebrows. 'Well, that's convenient,' she told him. 'The impossible is my speciality.'

'She's right, you know,' said a sudden voice in Mutt's ear, making him jump. Nissassa had moved silently to stand beside him. Together they watched

Clarity Jones revolving slowly in the middle of the room. She had placed the time trumpet back in the wooden chest and taken out a pair of strange glasses with bright red lenses. Wearing these, she was carefully examining every inch of the walls, her eyes narrowed in concentration.

A prickle ran down Mutt's back. A strange atmosphere seemed to fill the jester's bedroom, almost like a faint whisper telling him that something dreadful had happened here. The echoes of that peculiar ripping sound filled his brain. 'She will solve the mystery, won't she?' he asked Nissassa nervously.

'She's spent her whole life solving mysteries,' replied the assassin girl patronizingly. 'I hardly think a missing jester is going to be beyond her capabilities.'

'Who is she?' wondered Mutt out loud, still staring at Clarity Jones. The detective was now lying flat on the floor next to the jester's bed and was closely examining a hair she had plucked from the floor. 'Where does she come from?'

'Now that,' replied Nissassa, 'is a long story.'

'Which you're not going to tell me?' guessed Mutt.

'Right in one,' the girl confirmed.

But although Mutt doesn't find out the answers to

his questions until much later in the story, where they provide a very satisfying dramatic moment, *you* don't have to wait quite so long. (As long as you promise to act surprised when Mutt finds out, because you wouldn't want to make him feel left out now, would you?)

The Tale of Clarity Jones

PART I

The Princess Who Wanted Pockets

nce upon a time there was a princess. (Boring start, I know, but stick with it ~ it gets better.)

The princess grew up in a castle with her father, who was a king, and her mother, who was a queen, and her six older brothers, who were all princes. (It was a high-achieving family.) The castle was huge. Well, they generally are. You don't get that many two up, two down castles. It was also very cold and very rambling and very brilliant, with winding passageways and spiral staircases and turrets with flags on them and everything. For any curious sort of person it was impossible not to want to explore ~ and the princess was a very curious person indeed.

'Can I explore the castle?' she asked her parents as soon as she was old enough.

'Impossible!' said the king. 'A princess can't go wandering around the castle on her own. Anything could happen.'

'That's exactly why I want to do it,' replied the princess reasonably.

'I'm not sure I'm such a fan of the word "impossible",' added her mother the queen. 'I think a princess should be able to do whatever she wants.'

And so the princess set out to explore the castle. And by the time she was three years old, she knew her way round every single inch, even the secret passageways that had been built deep into the walls by some forgotten and doubtless rather creepy ancestor. She also discovered the library, which was large and musty-smelling and equipped with those amazing ladders on wheels.

'I'm going to read all these books,' she announced.

'Impossible!' announced the crabby and crusty librarian.

'I'm still not sure I like that word,' said the queen, who he hadn't noticed in the doorway. 'I think the princess can do anything she sets her mind to.'

And so the princess began to work her way through the books in the library. While her older brothers were learning to dance and ride tricorns and sit politely through performances of traditional dance and all the other things princes have to do, the princess would sit for hours on end in the

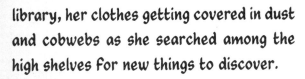

library, her clothes getting covered in dust and cobwebs as she searched among the high shelves for new things to discover.

A lot of people think that reading a lot of books gives you a great many answers. In fact, it gives you something far more useful. It gives you a great many questions. The princess loved all the books, but most of all she was fascinated by books about the magic that had once existed and had all but disappeared. Only a few magical items remained, the books told her, hidden carefully away or lost. 'I'm going to find as many missing magical artefacts as I can,' announced the princess.

'Impossible!' snapped the librarian, who thought that magic was much better left where it was, shut away on high shelves where it couldn't upset anyone.

'Mmm . . .' the princess replied.

When she was older still, a dressmaker arrived to make the princess look like an actual princess rather than a rather dusty servant. The princess looked at herself in the mirror, inspecting the flowing blue gown the dressmaker was sewing for her. 'It doesn't have pockets,' she pointed out. 'I need pockets. How am I going to carry a book, and a lantern for exploring, and a flint to light the lantern, and a knife, and all the other things I need, without pockets?'

'Impossible!' replied the dressmaker. 'Princesses' gowns don't have pockets.'

'You know what I think?' replied the princess thoughtfully, as she began to take off the gown. 'I think people are very fond of saying things are impossible, and in all my experience it's never actually been true.' And, of course, she was right. The word 'impossible' might sound very high and grand, like a mountain standing in your way, but different people react to mountains in different ways. Some turn round and go home. Others put on their climbing boots.

When she was older still, the princess realized something rather worrying. She

was now at the age when the rest of her life began to become a real proposition, and, being a princess, her career path was very much mapped out for her. She was supposed to smile, and wave, and wear pretty dresses, and eventually marry some dull prince, or at the very least an up-and-coming duke. And the princess realized that she really, really didn't want to do any of those things.

'I've been giving it a lot of careful thought,' she said to her father, the king, 'and I've decided that I'd like to give up being a princess, please. I'd like to explore the world and look for magic and solve puzzles.'

'Impossible!' said the king, going rather red in the face.

'I'm getting more than a little tired of that word,' said the queen.

'Me too,' agreed the princess. But this time the king dug his heels in. Exploring castles and reading books was one thing.

Going out into the world and looking for magic and solving mysteries was quite another. And he was the king, after all. So the princess carried on princessing, and steadily she grew more and more miserable.

A couple of years later, the story took an extremely sad turn, so prepare yourself. The queen fell dangerously ill, and despite calling in the best doctors in the kingdom, and then the best doctors in the Three Kingdoms, the king realized that the queen could not be saved. He gathered together his six sons and his daughter and they all stood round the queen's bedside.

'I want you to promise me something,' said the queen softly.

'Anything,' agreed the king, reaching out to gently hold her hand. And the queen looked across at her daughter and met her eye, and they both gave identical sad smiles.

'I want you to let her go,' the queen told

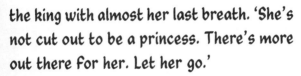

the king with almost her last breath. 'She's not cut out to be a princess. There's more out there for her. Let her go.'

'I can't lose both of you,' said the king. 'It's impossible!'

'You keep using that word,' replied the princess ~ whose name, by the way, was Clarity. 'I don't think it means what you think it means.'

And so, a few weeks after the queen's funeral, the king was forced to say farewell yet again, and he found it such a sad thing to do that he didn't get over it for many years. But when the princess stepped outside the castle one starlit night, wearing comfortable travelling clothes with an enormous number of pockets, she immediately felt a great weight lifting from her shoulders. Without looking back, she strode off into the warm summer darkness in search of magic and mystery. And she found a great deal of both.

CHAPTER 4

THE JESTER DETECTOR

In the bottom left-hand corner of Meandermart, or the south-west for the more geographically minded among you, was the cramped and dingy district known as the Assassins' Quarter. The streets were winding and poorly lit, because that's exactly the way assassins like things. And given that we're about to meet the mysterious villain of this story, you might expect that to be where the following scene is about to take place. But it doesn't. Because there's one thing that really good villains aren't, and that is predictable. So, instead of the Assassins' Quarter, the conversation upon which you're about to eavesdrop takes place among the wide, well-swept and neatly laid-out streets of the Merchants' Quarter. Here, large, tidy houses owned by large, tidy people stood proudly side by side, doing what they do best – looking like they cost a great deal of money. The Merchants' Quarter spread out to the south of Meandermart Castle, with the most expensive houses being those set on a slight hill near the castle causeway, with fine views of the great riverboats that clustered alongside the busy wharves.

Tucked away next to the towering city walls of Meandermart, built right up against the huge blocks of stone near to one of the old city gates, was a gigantic, rambling old mansion. It was one of the first ever to be built there, hundreds of years ago, and beneath the house was a deep cellar dug right beneath the walls. Even in the cold winter weather a week before Moaningtide, the cellar was warm, lit by the flickering light of a log fire that burned in a stone fireplace the size of a double bed. But, despite the close atmosphere, the visitor to the cellar that evening had not taken off his cloak. A deep hood kept his face in shadow (another hallmark of the successful villain: difficult to recognize) as he sat in a comfortable chair and stretched his boots out towards the fire.

'You're absolutely sure this will work?' said the visitor.

The man he was visiting sat in a chair opposite him, but in a much less relaxed position. This man, who was small and twitchy, leaned forward on the seat and rubbed his hands together constantly. 'It will work,' he reassured the visitor. 'Just a little longer and we will be able to make the exchange. Then the next phase of the plan should be much easier.' Behind the little man's chair, on the back wall of the cellar, stood a stout wooden door reinforced with thick bands of iron. And suddenly, from this door, there came a deep, sullen hammering noise. A few flakes of dust drifted down from the wooden ceiling. 'The creature is . . . difficult to control,' the man went on, rubbing his hands together harder. 'But I'm confident that it can be kept docile until the time is right.'

'It understands that it will be well rewarded?' the visitor asked, his eyes flickering towards the door.

'It does,' the man opposite him confirmed. He writhed in his chair, apparently wanting to say something further but too fearful to do so.

'Spit it out,' the visitor said contemptuously.

'They say the duchess has called in some woman to investigate,' the little man blurted all at once, sounding panicked. 'Called a detector or some such –'

'A detective,' the visitor corrected him smoothly. 'Never fear, my friend. This will work in my favour.'

'But what if she –' the small man began, before falling silent as suddenly as if a hand had been placed over his mouth. The tall man had held up a commanding finger as he rose from his chair.

'Silence,' he ordered. 'You just worry about making the transfer and keeping the creature under control. Leave this detective to me. She will soon wish she had never interfered.'

'I just can't find anything that fits,' complained Mirko, leafing through the pages of a small black book with a thick, furry finger. He leaned forward across the table and squinted. On the other side of the city, the Magical Detective Agency was working into the night on what the snow gnoblin was insisting they called the Mystery of the Flying Fool. Alongside his other duties, Mirko was the agency's official record-keeper, and when he wrote up his account of each case he very much liked to give it a snappy title. After they had returned from the castle, he had started leafing through the books that filled the shelves to one side of the shop, looking for clues. Well, not immediately. He had spent three hours heating up pails of water in front of the fire and filling a large bath, before washing his fur thoroughly clean of the mud that was still colouring his lower half. Then, after another couple of hours of careful combing, he had started his research. He now sat behind a table piled high with books, perched on a stool and hunched over uncomfortably as he pored over the pages.

'None of the best mysteries can be solved by a quick flick through a book,' reasoned Clarity Jones. The detective, like the mysterious visitor in the Merchants' Quarter, was sitting by the fire with her feet stretched out in front of her, gazing absently into the flames as she pondered.

'What is that book, anyway?' asked Nissassa, who was sitting in her usual position, tilted back on her chair, legs up on her desk beside the front door. She was sharpening one of her daggers – a long, slim blade with a carved ebony hilt – with a smooth black stone.

'I bought it from a sailor down the wharves,' Mirko replied, holding up the book and showing it to her. '*A Traveller's Guide to Rillia*,' he read from the title page. 'Some visitor wrote all this, ten years ago or more. Customs, people, creatures. I've been looking through the chapters on strange creatures, to see if there's anything that might have got up to the castle and attacked that jester. There's pages on gnangers, tricorns – all kinds of stuff. But not much that can fly. And nothing that could carry off a whole jester.'

'Two things I don't understand,' said Nissassa, with a tooth-panging scrape of her sharpening stone along the dagger. 'Firstly, why would anyone want to kidnap a jester? And secondly, why would they want him back? Unless you've found anything in his big book of jester jokes, street dog?' This last question was directed at Mutt, who sat on the floor with his back against the hearth, flicking through Handy Dandy's jester's handbook.

'Not unless you want to know a "moste risible methode for making ye rude noise with thy upper arme",' Mutt read aloud. 'There's three whole chapters on rude noises, actually.' Nissassa looked at him levelly without cracking a smile, and Mutt returned to the book, embarrassed. He was only here on a two-week trial, and he strongly suspected that if Nissassa had her way, he'd be out on his ear as soon as it was finished.

'You said there's *not much* that could carry something away,' said Clarity, moving over to Mirko's table and perching herself on the edge. 'Which sounds like there are *some* things.'

'Well, there's dragons, obviously,' the snow gnoblin replied. 'But we'd definitely know if one of them had come south. There are watchtowers every five miles all the way from here to the Draconian Wastes. Besides, I think a whole dragon flying up to the castle and grabbing a jester out of the window would have attracted somebody's attention.'

'What about a flyger?' asked Clarity. Mutt pricked up his ears. Like everyone else, he had heard stories of the huge striped cats with gigantic feathered wings that lived in the dense, hilly forests of Spess, the country to the south of Rillia. The Flyger Mountains were in the extreme west, a region known as Outer Spess, which was rarely visited and more than a little mysterious.

'Flygers don't interfere in our affairs,' the gnoblin replied. 'They keep themselves to themselves. And besides, they're kind, noble beasts. There's no reason for them to attack us here.'

'Well, what then?' asked Nissassa impatiently, spinning the dagger on its point and throwing it from hand to hand. 'Is there anything useful in that silly book?' Clarity Jones winced. She'd had a keen affinity with books since childhood and felt any insult to them rather personally.

'There's something useful in every book,' countered Mirko, earning himself a warm smile from the detective. 'This chapter's called "Creatures of the Truly Terrifying Forest",' the huge snow gnoblin went on. 'I was wondering whether something might have wandered out of the forest and made its way to the castle.'

Mutt felt a shiver on the back of his neck. Rillians stayed well clear of the Truly Terrifying Forest, which spread out to the north-east of Meandermart.

Every night when he returned to the boat-house, he could see the dark mass of the forest draped across the low hills. It always seemed to be shrouded in a chilly mist that clung to the gnarled branches of the tall, twisted trees with their dark trunks and permanently rustling leaves. Few dared to enter the gloom beneath the overhanging branches. There was one road that ran directly through the southern tip of the forest, which was known as the Gauntlet. Some of the more foolhardy young knights would occasionally get drunk and perform the dangerous ritual of 'running the Gauntlet', putting on their armour and dashing as fast as they could along the narrow, rutted track. Few of them ever made it out the other side – not in the same number of pieces they started out in, anyway. And those that did would never speak of what they'd seen inside the forest. They'd simply give a slight shiver and wish they'd chosen a less hazardous career – like mud-caked hermit guy – instead.

CREATURES OF THE TRULY TERRIFYING FOREST

UMLAUTS

*U*mlauts look exactly like clusters of leaves, except for their eyes, which glow in the dark. For this reason, an umlaut usually appears as two dots hovering above a tree branch.

If you ever see this pattern of dots, run away immediately before the umlaut attacks you with its highly poisonous talons.

NYTERRAS

*L*egendary shapeshifting creatures previously only found in the very deepest and most dangerous parts of the Truly Terrifying Forest. With their ability to assume the form of any other living creature, they used to represent a very real danger. Nyterras could fly great distances and there are numerous stories of nyterras taking the place of people, using their shapeshifting powers to infiltrate towns and villages before attacking the residents at night. Thankfully, nyterras are now extinct, the last one having been killed by the famous monster catcher Gabriel Ratchets over a decade ago. In their natural form, nyterras looked like giant leathery birds.

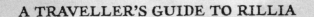

TAURCENTS

*H*alf human, half horse. But unfortunately the wrong halves. The taurcent's back legs are the legs of a man, but the front half of its body is formed of the back legs of a horse. This makes them extremely bad tempered, not to mention smelly.

GRABBITS

Grabbits hunt by burying themselves backwards in the forest floor with their mouths pointing up. If an unsuspecting traveller is unlucky enough to step into the resulting 'grabbit hole', the creature will immediately close its jaws, biting their foot off with razor-sharp teeth.

Clarity had moved behind Mirko to read over his shoulder. 'What about nyterras?' she asked, pointing at the book. 'They can fly. And they're easily big enough to carry off a jester.'

'What's a nyterra?' asked Mutt edgily. The word sounded ominous – a mixture of 'night' and 'terror' that made a slight chill edge along his hairline.

'Shapeshifters,' replied Mirko, reading. 'They look kind of like large lizards with huge bat wings.' He held the book up and Mutt got to his feet for a clearer view. He immediately wished he hadn't. On the page was a picture of a hideous-looking creature with a mean, beaked face and scaly skin. 'A nyterra can assume the form of another creature,' Mirko continued, turning the book back again to read the text, 'as long as it's spent sufficient time observing the subject. But they're extinct. Says here the last nyterra was killed by a monster catcher over ten years ago. Or there was something else –' he flicked forward again – 'oh yes, here you are. Giant moths. It says here the garganta moth is "native to the low hills on the fringe of the Draconian Wastes. They are carnivorous, and have been known to carry off animals as large as sheep or small dogs." Maybe a

CLARITY JONES AND THE MAGICAL DETECTIVE AGENCY

giant moth took the jester?'

'Why would a giant moth fly all the way here just to grab a jester?' countered Nissassa. 'That's ridiculous. He's a jester, not a candle. He's of no interest to a moth.'

'Well, if a flying creature didn't take him, what did?' said Mirko. 'I'm going to keep looking.'

'Could someone have climbed up and kidnapped him?' asked Clarity. 'You used to be an assassin, Nissassa – you know the way in and out of everywhere.'

'Nobody's ever climbed Meandermart Castle,' Nissassa told her. 'And plenty have tried, believe me.' She shook her head. 'Impossible.'

Clarity sighed. 'Perhaps we're coming at this from the wrong direction,' she said, getting up from the desk and beginning to pace the room. 'If we can't work out how Handy Dandy got out of the castle, maybe we should concentrate on something more important.'

'Which is?' asked Mirko, putting down the new book he'd just dragged from his pile.

'Where he is now,' Clarity told him. **'Smyll, come here! And, Mutt, give me that jester's book,** will you?' Mutt scrambled to his feet as the wooden chest cantered over, opening its lid. Clarity bent to retrieve a small square glass bottle. 'I haven't used this yet,' she said slightly doubtfully. 'But, in theory, it should work on any object that's been in close proximity to someone for a long time.'

'Well, the underduke said that Handy Dandy was always reading this,' Mutt pointed out helpfully.

'Exactly,' said Clarity, holding out her hand to take *Ye Jester's Companion* from him. Carefully, she tipped a few drops of a thick, golden liquid on to the cover. Instead of pooling on the brown leather, the drops disappeared with a tiny *plip* sound, as if they'd been poured into a bowl of water. And for a few seconds the entire book glowed a rich coppery gold. 'That seems to have worked,' said Clarity in a satisfied tone. 'Now, when this book is close to its former owner, it should glow again. Here you are –' she held it out – 'your first real test, Mutt. You want to be a detective? Go and detect something.'

Mutt took the book and looked at it questioningly. 'So, you want me to . . . what?' he said doubtfully. 'Just wander around the city with it until it lights up?'

'I want you,' said Clarity Jones, taking him by the

shoulders and spinning him to face the door, 'to go and do the thing that got you this trial in the first place. Go and look in some unexpected places.' With a gentle shove, she propelled him towards the door. 'Come straight back if that book does anything unexpected,' she told him. 'And, in the meantime, we'll keep looking into what might have taken him . . . and why.'

Mutt wasn't sure, but he was fairly certain that just before the door of the Magical Detective Agency closed behind him, he heard Nissassa say, 'Well, that should keep him out of the way for a bit.'

In many ways, Mutt's first task since he'd joined the Magical Detective Agency wasn't so very different from his life before he'd stumbled across their headquarters. For the next few days he wandered the streets of Meandermart just like before. But there were a few crucial differences that made his wanderings a little more comfortable. Firstly, he wasn't racing as fast as he could to try to make a few copper coins for a bowl of watery stew at the end of

the day. He still had the money pouch that Clarity Jones had given him, and he'd used it to make his life a little better in several ways. With only days to go until Moaningtide, the weather was bitter. But now Mutt had thick trousers, a cosy woollen jerkin and even a cloak. The boots that Underduke Ferdinand had given him did indeed fit perfectly, and the soft leather was sturdy yet comfortable. Most importantly, thanks to his pouch of coins, for the first time in years Mutt wasn't constantly hungry. In fact, when he'd bought a pie one afternoon, the goat-pie man had even given him a strange jerk of his face that might have been intended to serve as some kind of amateur version of a smile. Taking all this into account, it was small wonder that, as Mutt walked the streets three days later, there was a spring in his step and a glow in his tummy that hadn't been there before.

In between his searches, he'd spent many hours resting back at the Magical Detective Agency, sitting with his back against the stone hearth and half dozing while he listened to Clarity, Mirko and Nissassa discussing the case. But their conversations seemed to go round in circles. 'Who would want to get rid of a jester?' Clarity asked herself repeatedly.

'Everybody,' Nissassa replied every time. And Mutt would haul himself to his feet and head back out into the cold to continue his search.

But, after a full three days criss-crossing the city, Mutt had to admit to himself that he was beginning to run out of ideas. 'Look in unexpected places,' Clarity Jones had told him, and he'd been trying to do exactly that. He'd visited hidden squares and out-of-the-way gannicks that hardly anybody knew about. He'd zigzagged through the wide parkland that lay alongside the Oxbow Moat, with the cliffs beneath the castle towering above him. He'd crept through the city's graveyards, among moss-covered monuments of grey stone. But there had been no glimmer of light to show that *Ye Jester's Companion* was close to its former owner. It was beginning to look as if Handy Dandy had vanished from Meandermart altogether. *Perhaps Nissassa was right,* Mutt thought miserably to himself more than once. Perhaps Clarity was regretting giving him this trial at all, and had simply sent him off on a fool's errand to get him out of her hair while she got on with solving the case.

Mutt was, as usual, holding the small leather book out in front of him, watching it closely to see if it gave any vague hint of the golden glow he'd seen previously. So intently was he looking at it that he wasn't really paying much attention to where he was going. After years on the streets of Meandermart, it was not hard to amble around on autopilot, and he was fairly sure he'd covered nearly every street in the city already. But suddenly he heard a sound that made his insides feel like they were draining down into his legs.

'**Well, look who it is!**' said a confident braying voice. 'Looks like a certain little street dog has found a washing line to rob.'

Mutt stopped in his tracks, lowered the book and saw that he was right in front of the Knights' Academy. And the youths who had chased him the previous week were just filing out down the wide stone staircase that led from the front doors.

'Where did you get those clothes, dog?' asked another of the students, a tall girl with a freckled face and a superior expression. 'Who did you steal them from?'

'You know what I think?' said the first bully. 'I think it's our public duty as trainee knights to teach this little thief a lesson. And return those stolen clothes to their rightful owner.'

'They're not stolen!' Mutt, better fed and more confident than before, tried to stand his ground. 'I do not steal,' he said, echoing his parents' motto. But it was no use.

'Nonsense!' scoffed the freckled girl. 'You couldn't afford boots like that. **Get him!'**

Mutt, deciding that he wasn't going to be able to talk his way out of this one and resigning himself to yet another frenzied chase through the streets, took to his heels.

Up until the previous week, when the chase had ended with his stumbling into the Magical Detective Agency's HQ, these occasions had a depressing sense of déjà vu about them. The bullies from the Knights' Academy would eventually run Mutt to ground and give him a sound beating before dunking him in one of the many tricorn troughs that were scattered around the city. But today something was different. Several things, in fact. For a start, Mutt had now eaten properly for a few days, and he was wearing a pair of extremely high-quality boots. That being the case, the gang had difficulty keeping pace with him as he hared off towards the Mages' Quarter. But they were trainee knights – and you didn't get to be a proper knight without keeping yourself pretty fit. As Mutt rounded a corner, his breath steaming in the chilly air, he felt a hand pluck at his new cloak and realized they almost had him.

It was at that point that something strange occurred. Mutt was bracing himself for the cloak to be yanked backwards, pulling him off his feet and on to his back. But that didn't happen. Instead, there was a muffled *oomf* noise, not unlike a clanuna (a Rillian fruit similar to a melon) being hit with a wooden club, followed by a moist *splat*. Mutt stopped sprinting, a process that took a few seconds. By this time, his momentum had carried him some way further down the street, and when he turned he was surprised to see the freckle-faced girl who'd been about to grab him sitting down in a large and very uncomfortable-looking puddle. But instead of looking furious, or angry with herself for tripping, the girl looked absolutely terrified. And the reason for her terror was crouched down on one side of the puddle. It was a girl dressed all in black, with her hair piled atop her head in a complicated braid stuck through with the hilts of numerous daggers. One fist

was pressed to the muddy ground, the other was extended in a gesture that said, 'I just threw someone to the floor and I'm about to do it again.'

'Bullies, eh?' said Nissassa to the rest of the Knights' Academy students, who were standing round their fallen companion in an uneasy semicircle. 'I hate bullies. Someone tried to bully me once, and you know what happened to them?'

'No,' scoffed the girl with freckles, fixing the fierce newcomer with a scornful expression. Sure, she might be dressed like one of Meandermart's legendary assassins, but she was only about her own age. What harm could she possibly do?

'That's right,' replied Nissassa calmly, returning the freckled girl's gaze with a long, steely look. 'Nobody does. And by the way,' she added, 'get ready.'

'**Get ready for what?**' replied the ringleader, feeling Nissassa's stare pierce her like a dagger.

'**This,**' Nissassa replied. And, so fast that she seemed to blur in the cold morning light, she whirled forward, spinning on one hand and scissoring her legs. One by one, Mutt's pursuers began to hit the floor as their knees were kicked neatly out from under them. A few tried to ready themselves to fight back; one stocky boy raised his fists and took a swing at where Nissassa had been just a split second before. But his flailing punch met only air. Feeling a tap on his shoulder, he turned just in time to see a booted foot heading for his face. And that was the last thing he saw for a few minutes, apart from several stars as he hit the floor with a satisfying *splat*.

By the time Mutt had walked back down the street, Nissassa was dusting her hands together in a satisfied fashion, one foot on the chest of the freckled girl, who was now lying on her back in the puddle – a position that looked, if anything, even more uncomfortable than before. 'You weren't thinking of getting up, were you?' said Nissassa in a friendly tone. The girl sent out ripples of muddy water as she frantically shook her head. 'Excellent,' approved the retired assassin. 'Now listen, all of you. I am Nissassa of the White Hand Clan. You know what that means?' There was a splodging and a squelching as all the damp and horizontal knights-in-waiting nodded enthusiastically. 'This boy here is under my protection,' Nissassa continued, placing a firm hand on Mutt's shoulder. He was aware that he should be looking rather cool and capable at this point, but he was also aware that instead he was grinning like a complete idiot. To his surprise, he found that he didn't much care. 'So find someone else to chase.' Nissassa pushed her foot more firmly down on the ringleader. 'Got it?' There was another outbreak of frantic nodding from the floor. 'Very good.'

As they walked away, Mutt looked slightly nervously at the girl striding alongside him. Nissassa had never made much of a secret of the fact that she considered Mutt an unwelcome addition to the agency. Of all the team, she was the one who never tired of calling him 'street dog', the one who seemed to trust him the least.

'Erm . . . thanks,' he said to her awkwardly.

'Don't mention it.' Nissassa looked sideways at him. 'Like I said, I hate bullies.'

'Were you . . .' Mutt wasn't quite sure how to phrase this, but decided there really wasn't a polite way of saying it. 'Were you following me?'

'Yes,' she replied honestly. 'Well, checking in. I've been around and about the city, following up a few leads for Clarity. And I wanted to make sure you were carrying out your assignment. If there's one

CLARITY JONES AND THE MAGICAL DETECTIVE AGENCY

thing I hate more than bullies, it's someone who doesn't follow up on a promise.'

'**I was!**' Mutt plucked *Ye Jester's Companion* from his tunic and waved it at her. 'I've been walking around with this thing for days!'

'I know, I know.' Nissassa stopped and faced him, hands on hips. 'But I wanted to check. In all honesty, I wasn't quite sure that Clarity was right to take you on for this trial.'

'Yes.' Mutt gave her a crooked smile. 'I think you made that quite clear.'

'But you're doing your best,' Nissassa went on, as if she hadn't heard him. 'You've hardly stopped. You're trying your best not to let us down. And I must admit, you do seem to know the city fairly well. Almost well enough to be an assassin, in fact. I didn't think anybody else knew that alley behind the wharves that leads underneath the castle causeway.'

'The Hidden Jitty?' asked Mutt. 'Oh, yes! It's a great shortcut. And I won't let you down, I swear. I'll pass the trial,' he pledged, gripping the book tightly. 'I'll walk every street in the city until this thing starts glowing.'

'You really want to join us?' Nissassa stopped and

faced him, hands on her hips again and her face screwed up into a sceptical expression.

'Of course!' An image of the Magical Detective Agency's shop flashed into Mutt's mind with a warm flood of affection. He saw Mirko bent over his books, and Clarity rummaging inside Smyll for some fantastical device, potion or powder. And he saw the girl who was now standing opposite him toying with a dagger behind her desk. 'I guess . . . I guess I'm looking for a family,' he told her uncertainly.

Nissassa snorted. **Strange sort of family!'**

'Aren't they the best kind, though?'

And at this, Nissassa gave him the briefest of smiles, just a flash of sunlight between scudding clouds. 'You know what? I think you might have a point there . . . Mutt.' And, even though it was only a nickname that he'd been given on the streets of Meandermart, the way she said it somehow made it sound like a mark of respect.

The Tale of Clarity Jones

Part II

The Monsters of the Mountains

nce upon a time there was a warrior.

This warrior was a snow gnoblin, and he came from a proud family of great warriors, some of the most famous in the huge snowy expanse of the Great Southern Mountains. As he grew up, it quickly became obvious that he was unusually large and strong, even among his own people. The whole clan was convinced that he would go down in history as one of the truly great gnoblin warlords.

The problem was, this snow gnoblin, whose name was Mirko, didn't especially like fighting. He found it a rather messy business, and Mirko really, really hated mess. Fighting made him all sweaty and matted his fur. If he got knocked to the ground during a battle, it took him ages to get the mud out afterwards. What he really liked doing was sitting by the fire in the huge cavern where his clan lived, reading some of the books that had been passed down through his family.

149

As you can imagine, Mirko was something of a disappointment to the other snow gnoblins. Their chief interests were hunting, and fighting, and roaring, and feasting on roasted meats. Mirko didn't really enjoy any of these things, especially not the roasted meats, which made his hands all greasy. But he took part in all of it because he lived in the mountains and there really wasn't much choice.

One day, Mirko and the other members of his clan were out on a hunting expedition. They were searching for slaughs, which are a little like gigantic white bears only with long, floppy ears and long teeth that are the opposite of floppy. Slaughs are extremely bad tempered and extremely dangerous and extremely delicious when you put them on a spit over an open fire ~ hence the hunting party. This particular day, the clan ran an unusually large slaugh to earth in a narrow, rocky valley. There was a great battle, during which Mirko was gouged in the leg by one of the slaugh's

razor-sharp teeth. It was very painful and, worse than that, the blood had soaked into his white fur.

'Look at this,' he told his clan-mates. 'That's going to be a nightmare to clean.' They rolled their eyes behind his back.

'Wait here,' the clan chief told him. 'You can't walk on that leg. We'll take the beast back to the cavern and return to fetch you.' They led him into a shallow cave in the valley side and sat him down on a boulder.

'See you in a bit, then!' shouted Mirko as the rest of the clan, carrying the dead slaugh, disappeared back down the mountain. He thought he heard one of them laugh as they vanished round a bend in the path.

'I'm not entirely sure,' said Mirko to himself glumly, 'but I think I've been abandoned on this mountain to freeze to death. Without a comb, too. Typical.'

And that might have been the very sad end to the story of this huge, kind and

151

cleanliness-loving snow creature. But, luckily, the snow gnoblin clan were not the only beings braving that part of the Great Southern Mountains that particular day. There was a traveller, too. A traveller wrapped tightly in a blue cloak.

This traveller was now going by the name Clarity Jones. She'd decided that the title 'princess' would attract quite a lot of unwanted attention now that she'd given up the princessing part of her life. She'd left her home far, far to the north on her eighteen-and-a-halfth birthday with nothing but a wooden chest, and had gone in search of magic and mysteries. She'd travelled south, through the kingdom of Spess, all the way to the kingdom of Informatia. There, she had pored over countless books in the great libraries before setting out on a long journey to discover hidden pieces of magic. This journey had now been going on for three years, and it had been a huge success. It turned out that the former princess had a real nose for sniffing out magical artefacts. She found them hidden in all sorts of places, and she was starting to amass quite a collection.

Mirko didn't know any of this, of course. He only knew that he was cold and couldn't walk, and his clan had abandoned him, and his leg fur was all matted with dried blood. It had turned into a really rubbish Wednesday, to be honest. So, when he heard footsteps on the high mountain pass, he simply assumed his day was about to get even worse. 'I'm in here,' he said in a resigned tone of voice. 'Come on, you may as well eat me. I'll only freeze to death in a couple of hours anyway. Let's get it over with . . .' But instead of a monster of some kind, what actually appeared round the corner was a wooden chest, running on four stubby legs, followed by a tall woman in a blue cloak.

'Hello,' said the woman. 'My name's Clarity Jones. I'm a traveller.' (This was in the days before she invented the word 'detective' of course.)

'My name's Mirko,' said Mirko. 'I'm a snow gnoblin warrior, and I rather suspect I've been left here to die on this mountain.'

'And do you want to do that?' asked the traveller.

'I'm fairly keen not to, actually.'

'Because you could come with me instead, if you want, and travel the world looking for magic and mysteries. You'd have to leave the mountains behind, though. I'm heading north, back towards my homeland.'

'Mmm.' Mirko thought for a moment. 'How muddy is it likely to be?' he asked.

'Pretty muddy, if I'm being honest,' replied Clarity Jones.

'That's not ideal,' the snow gnoblin admitted. 'But it still sounds better than freezing to death. I'm in.'

'Excellent,' replied Clarity. 'Here, Smyll!' The wooden chest gambolled up to her, opening its lid. And she sprinkled a green

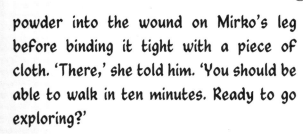

powder into the wound on Mirko's leg before binding it tight with a piece of cloth. 'There,' she told him. 'You should be able to walk in ten minutes. Ready to go exploring?'

'I just need to pop home quickly,' said Mirko. 'I need to fetch a couple of things. Oh, and beat up my clan members really quite badly for leaving me behind like that.'

And then, once those two objectives had been achieved, the warrior left his home behind forever and set out into the world with his new family. It was huge and fascinating, but unfortunately even muddier than he could possibly have imagined.

CHAPTER 5

MULLED WHINE AND LAMENTATIONS

Mutt was not a boy who gave up easily. He hadn't given up after the death of his parents. He hadn't given up after being constantly chased round the streets of Meandermart by the students of the Knights' Academy. He hadn't given up after eating nothing but watery stew for months on end. He hadn't given up after living all alone for years. One missing jester certainly wasn't going to change that.

And, he mused to himself one evening, as he sat on the ledge overlooking the sluggish waters of the River Rill, things had slowly started to improve. Thanks to that one wrong turn, he had been led by chance to Clarity Jones's door. Thanks to Nissassa, the Academy students seemed to have given up on him. He'd run into a couple of them a few days after her attack, and they'd quickly hurried off in the other direction, muttering anxiously to each other and casting nervous glances towards nearby windows. Thanks to Clarity's purse of coins, he had feasted on goat pie every single day – he'd even caught himself wondering whether he might fancy something different for a change. And, perhaps most importantly, he no longer felt so alone. Everyone at the Magical Detective Agency really was starting to feel, if not like family, then at least like a group of good friends who he could turn to if he needed help. It was an unfamiliar feeling, nestling deep inside him like a tiny flickering fire, and he was almost afraid to examine it too carefully in case the fresh air put it out.

Despite all this, the Mystery of the Flying Fool was proving a tough case to crack. Clarity and the others seemed to be largely relying on Mutt pounding the streets with *Ye Jester's Companion*. 'He must be somewhere,' the detective said to Mutt every morning. 'If I've discovered one thing on my travels, it's this: nothing's ever lost forever. People said magic was lost, and I managed to track down quite a lot of it.' She gestured towards Smyll, dozing peacefully on the hearth. 'It's always somewhere,' she insisted. 'Just keep looking.'

'How do you know he's not just left the city completely?' grumbled Mirko from his desk. 'It's been over a week by now. He could be halfway to Informatia – or more, if he actually did fly out of the window.'

'He's still in Meandermart,' replied Clarity Jones, scratching her nose. 'I can feel it right here.' And that seemed unanswerable.

And so, for day upon day, Mutt crossed and re-crossed the city, racking his brains for any hidden jitty or gannick that he might have forgotten to check. And then, one afternoon (you'll be relieved to hear), just as he was beginning to think there was no tiny corner of Meandermart he hadn't checked, he accidentally cracked the case wide open. And this is how it happened.

It was late afternoon, and candlelight glowed from the windows. Mutt could see that most houses had now put up their Moaningtide trees. Dead branches hung with greyish pieces of parchment upon which folk had written their least favourite things about winter. On the street corner, he passed a crowd of people holding lanterns on sticks and singing a traditional Moaningtide gripe:

Everybody's ill and wheezing,
Fiddle diddle dee, dee dum dum dee.
My hands and feet are chuffing freezing,
Fiddle diddle dee, dee dum dum dee.
How I wish that it was summer,
Fiddle dee, fiddle dee, dum dum dee.
Winter is a total bummer,
Fiddle diddle dee, dee dum dum dee.

(You'll have to make up your own tune, but you get the idea.)

Mutt was quietly singing along as he trudged past the gripers and on through the Merchants' Quarter, snug in his new boots and cloak. The cold air was fragrant with the scent of baking as people prepared the small cakes called lamentations or made steaming pots of spiced mulled whine.

'Miseries of the season to you, young master!' called out an old woman from an open window.

'I am so cold and hating every second of it.' Mutt gave the traditional response without thinking. Just then, a glint caught the corner of his eye. *Ye Jester's Companion*, clutched tightly in his left hand as always, had given a faint flicker. Excitedly, Mutt realized that although he'd walked up and down this street several times over the past few days, he'd always been on the other side of the road. The gripers had forced him into a slight detour, and this had brought him close to the large houses along the city wall. Barely breathing, he pulled the book fully out from under his cloak and spun on the spot, watching it intently. Sure enough, as he faced this side of the street, the book gave another glimmer of golden light. With a whoop of delight quite out of keeping with the dismal Moaningtide atmosphere, Mutt dashed off towards the Mages' Quarter to give the news that he, Clarity's new assistant, had just made a breakthrough. Surely he'd be taken on as a proper apprentice now!

By the time he arrived back at the Magical

Detective Agency, he was out of breath and his new boots and cloak, rather than being snug, were extremely hot and uncomfortable. He burst through the door and stood panting in the centre of the room, holding *Ye Jester's Companion* aloft but unable to speak for a moment as he panted frantically.

'Oi!' said Mirko, getting up from his chair and pointing angrily downwards. 'You've walked filth in here again!' Mutt looked at his boots and saw that they were, indeed, caked in chilly mud the colour and texture of chocolate mousse. 'I'll get the mop,' grumbled the gnoblin, tutting and throwing his eyes to the ceiling as he stumped off towards the cupboard.

'Meh,' panted Mutt, still unable for the moment to get out any actual coherent words. 'Neff. Grah!' He shook the book frantically, widening his eyes.

'I think the little fella's trying to tell us something,' said Nissassa. She somersaulted nimbly over her desk and came to stand in front of Mutt. 'What is it, boy?' she asked sarcastically, as if he were an excited dog. 'Did you want to say something?'

'**Yaff,**' agreed Mutt, sucking in a huge lungful of air.

'Clarity,' called Nissassa. 'I think this little street

dog has found something. Come on, boy,' she said, nodding encouragingly, 'tell us what it is and I'll find you a nice biscuit.'

'**Stop teasing him,**' came a voice from behind Mutt. Clarity Jones was standing in the doorway, her eyes shining with excitement. 'What happened?' she asked Mutt gently. 'Did the book light up?'

And, with a final giant inhalation, the exhausted Mutt regained the power of speech. 'The book lit up,' he confirmed.

'Told you,' said Clarity to Nissassa, who gave a reluctant shrug of the shoulders. 'Let's go and get that jester,' she added to Mirko, who was making himself busy with the mop and foaming bucket.

'Can't it wait?' the snow gnoblin complained, plonking the bucket down. 'This'll be easier to clean if I do it while it's wet,' he reasoned, waving a clawed hand at Mutt's footprints.

'It can't wait!' Clarity told him. And, with a swish of her blue cloak, she led them all out of the door and away, Mirko having to leave in such a hurry that he completely forgot to put down the mop.

Half an hour later, Mutt was leading the others back down the same neat, wide street in the

Merchants' Quarter, holding Handy Dandy's favourite book out like a torch in front of him. Sure enough, as they approached the same spot, the golden glow reappeared.

'Right,' said Mirko, flexing his enormous arms. 'Looks like it's that house over there.' He pointed to an imposing residence on the other side of the street, set right back against the city wall. 'Hold this,' and he thrust the mop into Clarity's hands.

'We could just knock?' suggested Clarity, but it was too late. The snow gnoblin had marched across the road, his feet cracking the ice on the puddles and sending gobbets of muddy water up the white fur on his legs, and approached the stout double doors on the front of the house. Without pausing, he raised both his fists as if about to knock, but instead simply pushed the wooden doors. They came off their hinges with a shriek of tortured metal and crashed to the floor inside. Before the dust had settled, Nissassa had somersaulted through the opening, dropping into a crouch and scanning the room for any possible danger.

Luckily, the room contained nothing except a jester, so there was no danger other than that of mild irritation. Jesters really are quite annoying.

The jester in question was tied to a chair in the middle of the room. There was a gag over his mouth. And, tempting though it might have been to leave it there, Clarity reluctantly decided to remove it. 'Handy Dandy, I presume?' she asked politely as she untied it, the bells on the jester's floppy hat jingling gently as she did so.

'No,' the jester replied with a sarcastic snarl. 'I'm actually the Overqueen of the Three Kingdoms. Untie me, you idiotic woman. **Of course I'm Handy Dandy.'** He tutted angrily.

Nissassa leaped over, her eyes flashing with rage. 'You'd do best to keep a civil tongue in your head, jester,' she said quietly, her hand on the hilt of her third-favourite dagger, the one she kept strapped to her left thigh. 'We've spent the past week scouring the city for you.'

'Well, bravo.' Now that his hands were free, Handy Dandy was able to give a slow, sarcastic handclap. 'Congratulations on finally finding me. Now, shall we get to the castle? You don't want to waste any more time, I presume?'

'That jester is far more mean and sarcastic than I'd expected,' said Mirko to Mutt as Handy Dandy rose from his chair and rubbed his yellow-and-red-clad arms and legs to restore the circulation. 'I was preparing myself for a lot of "Folderol, nuncle, forsooth!" – that's the kind of stuff they normally do.'

'Maybe he's, like, an alternative jester?' suggested Mutt uncertainly.

'Hurry up, you jabbering poltroons,' snarled Handy Dandy. 'The duchess needs me back in time for the state visit. Stop whispering to each other and escort me to her. Immediately!'

'Do you think the duchess would be annoyed if we beat him up slightly before taking him back?' asked Nissassa hopefully, hand still on the dagger.

'I rather think she would, sorry,' replied Clarity, frowning. 'Who took you?' she asked Handy Dandy, looking at him intently. 'How did you get out of the castle?'

'There's no time for questions now, you

bimbling wastrel!' snapped the jester sourly, shaking his head so the bells on his cap jingled once again. 'Escort me to the duchess with all possible speed!'

'Yes, I can see why she'd be missing his hilarious banter,' said Mirko under his breath as they filed out of the house, Clarity leading the way, and turned right towards the castle.

'And why on earth are you carrying a mop, you idiot?' the jester snarled as they went.

Clarity, who had almost forgotten she was holding it, turned to Mirko. 'Mind if we leave this behind?' she asked him. 'I don't really want to turn up at the castle holding a mop.'

'Leave it behind? Leave Molly behind?' he repeated, his voice high with indignation. 'Don't worry,' he said softly to the mop. 'I'd never leave you behind.'

'Did you actually call it Molly the Mop?' asked Nissassa, as they jogged slightly to keep up with Handy Dandy. (The jester was marching through the chilly streets at a brisk pace with the Magical Detective Agents trailing after him.)

'So what if I do?' retorted Mirko. 'You've got names for all your daggers.'

'That's different,' said the assassin with a sniff.

'Stop your pathetic jabbering!' snapped Handy Dandy from up ahead. 'You're giving me a headache!'

'Yep, he really isn't very funny, is he?' mused Nissassa. 'What's going on, Clarity? Ever met such a bad-tempered jester before?'

'I have not,' the detective replied, staring thoughtfully at Handy Dandy's back as he led them towards the castle causeway, the bells on his hat jingling with each stride. 'And it really doesn't seem right.' She reached up and scratched her nose absent-mindedly. 'In fact,' she went on softly, almost to herself, 'something here seems very, very strange indeed. It's almost as if . . .' She trailed off.

'What is it?' asked Mutt, overhearing. A sudden chill ran down his spine as the castle loomed above them in the early-evening gloom. 'What's wrong?'

'I don't know yet,' said Clarity. 'But one thing is for certain.' There was a shout from the battlements and a creaking as the gates were opened to admit them. 'I have a bad feeling about this.'

CHAPTER 6

BETRAYAL, BANISHMENT AND OTHER BAD STUFF

'My noble lady.' Handy Dandy swept off his jester's hat and, extending one leg forward across the throne room floor, swept into an elaborate bow. 'I return to you.'

Duchess Peruka was beaming. She would have jumped for joy if her enormous wig hadn't rendered that completely impossible. Her jester was back, just in time for the arrival of her very important guests. And the guests really were very important. One of them was, in fact, the King of Rillia, and it didn't get much more important than that. The jester's act, where he would caper among the crowd telling seasonal jokes and making rude noises with various animal parts, would form the main part of the Moaningtide banquet, now only two days away. The thought of holding an actual banquet for an actual king without a jester had been enough to make her break out in a sweat. She was already sweating quite a lot because of the gigantic wig, but you know. It would have been complete social death. The king might even have left in a huff – and when that happens you know you've thrown a really, really unsuccessful party.

'Handy Dandy,' she said, rising slowly to her feet. The wig-supporting servant, with a slight roll of his eyes, followed suit, tensing his arms on the wig pole and preparing for another spell of agonizing bicep burn. 'I'm so delighted to see you. You return to us just in time. And I trust that our city's finest, er, "detective" . . . ?' She tested out the still-unfamiliar word. 'I hope she has solved the mystery? Doubtless some jealous noble who wanted my Moaningtide banquet to be a failure, I imagine?' Once again she felt a hot flush pass across her scalp at the very thought.

'Actually, despite returning the jester, I don't really feel I've solved the mystery, Your Marvellousness,'

Clarity replied, gesturing apologetically and realizing she was *still* holding Mirko's favourite mop. 'Hold this,' she told Mirko, thrusting it behind her before turning back towards the throne. But Duchess Peruka wasn't really paying attention. She had tottered down the steps, the wig-supporting servant labouring behind her, and was fussing over Handy Dandy like a mother hen, smoothing down his colourful costume and rubbing a smudge off his cheek. The jester looked as if he was about to stop her for a moment, but quickly plastered a sickly and rather fake-looking smile over his face and simpered unconvincingly. Clarity Jones's frown deepened. 'There's so much here I still don't understand,' she said out of the corner of her mouth to the other members of the Magical Detective Agency.

'What's the problem?' replied Nissassa in a stage whisper. 'We returned the jester. We'll get paid. On to the next case!'

'I didn't become a detective just to get paid,' Clarity told her, scratching her head. 'I wanted to solve puzzles. And we still don't know what happened.'

Mutt could feel the frustration radiating out from Clarity like a heat haze, but he was struggling with some very mixed feelings. On the one hand, he was delighted that his careful search of Meandermart's winding streets had led to the discovery of the jester's location. But, on the other, his brain burned with the unanswered questions that, as if she could read his mind, Clarity was now listing.

'How did he get out of the castle without opening the door? Who took him? And why? You know,' Clarity said, 'I'm beginning to think that there's a lot more to this case than meets the eye. There's something I just can't put my finger on. Something . . .'

'Impossible?' replied Mutt, widening his eyes.

'**Exactly!**' They exchanged a serious glance. 'The Mystery of the Flying Fool –' Clarity began, but before she could say any more she was cut off by something so completely unbelievable that it left her utterly unable to draw breath for a moment.

Handy Dandy's voice suddenly rang out through the throne room, raised to a harsh shout. 'Before you thank this woman, Your Marvellousness,' said the jester, lifting himself up to his full height (which was not particularly high, for the record) and moving a few steps towards the detective, 'I think I should reveal the shocking truth. Prepare yourselves, my lords and ladies –' he waved an arm to take in the nobles who were hanging around the throne room as usual instead of having proper jobs to go and do – 'because I am about to reveal something that will make each particular hair on your head stand on end, like the quills of the fretful porpentine.'

At this, the assembled lords and ladies all craned their necks forward. If there was one thing they loved in their largely empty lives, it was a bit of drama. And this was already much more entertaining than Handy Dandy's usual routine. Fewer bodily noises and head-hitting, for a start. Even if none of them was completely sure what a porpentine was.

'She tried to fool me with a cunning disguise,' the jester went on. 'But I knew her voice at once. This woman –' he pointed dramatically at Clarity Jones – 'this woman is the very person who abducted me from the castle! She spirited me away in the dead of night and imprisoned me in her house!'

There was a gasp, and every single pair of eyes looked at Clarity Jones. Most of them in horror, but the eyes of Mutt, Nissassa and Mirko held only disbelief and confusion.

'What in Rillia are you going on about, you silly little man?' said Nissassa furiously. Clarity was still speechless, staring at the jester with narrowed eyes and looking as if she was thinking very hard and very, very fast.

'Silence, assassin!' spat Handy Dandy. 'Learn to keep a civil tongue in your head in the presence of the duchess.'

'He really is not that funny, is he?' Mirko said to Mutt out of the corner of his mouth, gripping the handle of Molly the Mop tightly in both anger and confusion.

'*What* is the meaning of this?' Duchess Peruka rose up to her full height, causing her wig servant to stand precariously on tiptoe.

'I think I might be able to explain, dear sister,' said a new voice. Mutt breathed a sigh of relief as Underduke Ferdinand stepped forward from his customary place to one side of the throne. Surely, Mutt thought, this friendly young man was about to speak up on their behalf. But, unbelievably, that wasn't what happened. 'I think this so-called detective has made a not-very-cunning plan to try to build her reputation,' the underduke went on, pacing in front of Clarity and regarding her with a rather pitying expression. 'It seems she decided to abduct our beloved Handy Dandy, knowing that we would call on her services to try to find him.'

'Lies!' Nissassa sprang forward, but Clarity placed a calming hand on her arm. Nissassa had been forced to leave her weapons at the Strangers' Tower, as before, on their way up to the castle. (Molly the Mop had been reluctantly allowed to pass.) But even without her array of daggers, throwing stars and other assorted metalware, the girl assassin could have made life extremely uncomfortable for the underduke with her fingers alone. Clarity Jones held her back, though.

'We need to understand what's going on here,' the detective whispered. 'That's never going to happen if we all end up in the dungeons. You need to get out of here.'

'Unfortunately for her, her plot has failed,' went on Ferdinand. His eyes passed briefly over Mutt, who was looking at him in anger and disbelief, but he gave no sign he'd noticed.

'**Treason!**' Duchess Peruka was trembling with fury. '**Guards! Take her to the dungeons immediately! The rest of you –**' her blazing eyes landed on Mirko, Nissassa and Mutt – '**you are banished from the castle forthwith! You are forbidden ever to enter these walls again, on pain of death!**'

'You'll regret this!' Nissassa's eyes flashed as she moved forward, but once again, Clarity Jones held her back.

'You need to leave,' she urged the girl. '**Go! Get out of here!** And work out what's really happening. I know you want to fight –'

'I don't want to *fight*,' Nissassa broke in. 'I just want to rip off that soppy underduke's head, then rip off that grumpy jester's head, and make them into a pair of novelty maracas. There won't be any fighting involved.' But, before she could put her threat into action, she felt a tug on her black leather sleeve. Mutt was by her side.

'Clarity's right,' he told her. 'We need to solve the case. Properly solve it. We won't understand what's going on otherwise.'

By now, the whole team, including Molly the Mop, were surrounded by burly castle guards. Clarity's hands had been roughly pulled behind her back and she was being dragged out of the throne room as Handy Dandy watched with a sinister grin. Just before she was hustled out of a side door, the detective managed a brief shout to her fellow agents: 'Find out what happened to Handy Dandy!' she urged them. And at this point her eyes met Mutt's. 'Remember what I said just now,' she told him. 'It's im–' But at that point the door slammed closed behind her.

Mutt felt a sharp metal pike pushing uncomfortably into his back as he, Nissassa and Mirko were forced towards the main doors.

'This is madness!' Nissassa was yelling. 'You're being lied to! We're innocent!'

'Exactly what a guilty person would say, my noble lady,' Handy Dandy told the duchess with an extra-oily leer in their direction.

'It seems Meandermart is better off without an, um, a *detective* after all,' added Underduke Ferdinand, giving his sister a comforting pat on the arm as the castle doors slammed shut, locking Mutt and his friends outside. 'Now, how about a cup of comforting mulled whine? And we'll summon the minstrels to sing some of your favourite gripes,' he went on. 'You just forget all about those criminals, and we'll prepare for the feast. After all, the king will be here tomorrow.'

And the duchess, much to the relief of the wig-holder, sank back on to her throne, pleased that this dastardly plot had been revealed to her. And Handy Dandy, with one last secret smile, which looked more than a little evil if you were close enough to see it properly, settled himself on the top step right beside the throne and gazed at her intently and, if we're being completely honest, incredibly creepily.

'I'll kill that jester!'

Nissassa was still raging as Mirko and Mutt half led (Mutt) and half carried (Mirko) her through the door of the Magical Detective Agency's shop and plonked her down on the comfortable chair by the fire.

'Ooh, that double-crossing, sneaky, stupid-hatted, bad-tempered little –' Luckily for us, the last word was drowned out by Mirko slamming the door shut and stumping across the room to rake the embers back into life and throw a log into the fireplace.

'I just don't understand it,' the huge gnoblin said thoughtfully as flames began to flick around the dry wood. 'We know full well that Clarity wasn't involved –'

'Of course she wasn't involved!' interrupted Nissassa angrily. 'How can you even *say* that?'

'I thought we were supposed to consider absolutely everything?' replied Mirko mildly. 'We've got a mystery on our hands here. We're not going to solve it by ranting and raging. And the sooner we solve it, the sooner we can get Clarity out of those dungeons.'

'I'm not just going to rant and rave,' said Nissassa, with an icicle-tip sharpness in her tone. 'I'm going to get inside that castle, armed to the teeth, and start slicing parts off that Handy Dandy until he tells me what's going on. And then for good measure I'm going to stick something very sharp and very uncomfortable into that stupid floppy-haired Ferdinand. Why did he turn on us like that?'

'That,' said Mirko thoughtfully, 'is a truly excellent question. And one that needs a lot of thought.'

'Oh, *thought*.' Nissassa curled her lip at him scornfully. 'That's your answer to everything, isn't it? The only thing I'm going to think about is how to get into that castle with as many daggers as I can carry.'

'Nobody's ever got inside Meandermart Castle,' Mirko told her. 'You said it yourself: it's impossible.'

'Well, I'll wait until he comes out for a walk then,' said Nissassa desperately. 'Then I'll ambush him . . .' She slumped back in the chair, muttering plans to herself in which the words 'dagger', 'impale' and 'pancreas' featured heavily.

Mutt, meanwhile, had wandered over to his favourite spot by the hearth and had sunk to the ground. Ever since he'd stumbled into this room by accident, his life had changed in ways he'd never have been able to imagine barely two weeks ago. And now, just when he'd been expecting to enjoy a moment of triumph at a puzzling case solved, it had all come crashing down. He just couldn't understand it. Why had Handy Dandy turned on them like that? It seemed clear that the jester must have been involved in his own mysterious disappearance, but how? And why had he pinned the blame on Clarity Jones like that? And how had he really managed to vanish from one of the castle's highest towers?

'There's something about that jester that really bothers me,' said Mirko softly, as if echoing Mutt's thoughts. 'And not just the fact that he was really, really not funny.'

'Everyone who's met Handy Dandy said he was kind of annoying,' said Mutt, catching the snow gnoblin's eye and exchanging a look of puzzlement. 'But nobody said anything about him being so mean and sarcastic, did they? I wonder what happened?'

'Who cares what happened?' Nissassa rose from her chair, fists clenched. 'What is this, a "feel sorry for the grumpy jester club"? Because I am so not here for that.'

'We're just trying to solve the mystery –' Mutt began, but she cut him off.

'I don't know what you're still doing here anyway!' she shouted, kicking out at him with a black boot. 'You found that stupid jester! It's your fault we're in this situation in the first place! It's your fault Clarity's in prison!' Her voice quavered. 'There's nothing more you can do here. We don't have a detective, so there can't be an apprentice. So . . . so I think you can assume your trial period is at an end.'

Mutt rose to his feet in alarm, and Mirko started to protest, but she silenced him with an angry wave of her arm. 'Just get out,' she told Mutt, her face a mixture of fury and sadness. 'Go home, street dog. There's nothing more you can do.' And Mutt, feeling as if his insides had turned into cold, dirty dishwater, slunk out of the door without another word and disappeared into the winding streets of Meandermart like a raindrop vanishing into the sea.

The dungeons were located in the deepest, dingiest catacombs set into the cliffs beneath Meandermart Castle. This is a fairly standard dungeon placement;

castle designers have always tended to favour a basement position, just as they pick the largest, most impressive spot for the throne room (see Chapter 3). The catacombs were reached by a series of increasingly narrow, damp and treacherous staircases cut into the bare rock itself, and, as Clarity Jones was bundled down these steps by several burly guards, she could feel the air growing colder and danker as the sounds of the castle above echoed, receded and then vanished altogether. By the time she reached the dungeon level, the only sound was the padding of boots on wet stone, the clanking of the guards' armour and their panting breaths as they hurried their captive towards her cell.

Rounding a corner in the lowest staircase, they came to a wide opening set in the wall. Behind this hatch sat a huge mountain gnoblin, his bare white skin seeming almost to glow in the dim atmosphere of the dungeons. The stubby horns on his head glinted as he looked up curiously from the book he was writing in with a quill.

'Ah, good afternoon,' said the gnoblin in a friendly, cultured voice. 'Checking in?'

Clarity Jones was rather nonplussed by this. In her

wide and lengthy travels, she'd been unfortunate enough to end up in a few dungeons, and nobody had ever politely asked her if she was 'checking in'. The script was usually more along the lines of, 'Mwahahaha! Abandon all hope, prisoner, for none hath ever escaped from these dreary cells with their sanity intact. Mwahahaha!'

'I'm sorry?' she asked, deciding to play for time until she could work out what she was dealing with.

'I said, are you checking in?' the huge white-skinned figure repeated. 'Checking in to the dungeons? You've been imprisoned, yes?'

'Erm, yes, that's right,' replied Clarity uncertainly.

'Splendid.' The gnoblin nodded to the guards before bending to scribble something in his book. 'Afternoon, Norman. Hello, Samantha – how's your rockery coming along?' The larger of the guards gave a brief grunt in reply. 'Splendid. Good to hear it. Now then, let me see . . .' He ran a stubby finger down a list of names. 'Number twelve is free, I think. Single room, all amenities and a lovely view. Yes, we'll put you in twelve. Just let me find your key.' The gnoblin spun round on his chair to inspect a series of oversized black metal keys hanging neatly on hooks on the wall behind him. 'Here we are,' he continued in a sing-song tone, grabbing a key and getting to his feet. He disappeared from behind the hatch, then reappeared a moment later out of a wooden doorway on to the passageway, plucked a flaming torch from the wall and beckoned to the guards. Grabbing Clarity roughly by the arms, they hustled her after the unusually polite turnkey as he led them further into the dungeons.

'**Help me, please!**' wailed a voice as Clarity passed one of the barred doors that punctuated the corridor on either side. '**I can't stand it any more!**'

'Don't worry, that's Horace,' explained the gnoblin over his shoulder. 'One of our longest-serving residents. You'll soon get used to him. Oh, forgive me – I didn't introduce myself, did I? How rude. My name's Bayler. I'll be looking after you during your time here in the dungeons. Which will be until you die, of course. Haha.' He gave a polite little laugh and continued to lead the way, the orange torchlight bobbing on the damp, cold walls.

'Sorry, just to be clear,' said Clarity, 'your name's Bayler, and you're the jailer?'

'Yes.' The gnoblin stopped and half turned,

looking puzzled.

'It's just that it rhymes,' Clarity pointed out.

'Does it?' The gnoblin's horns caught the torchlight as he threw back his head in thought.

'Bayler . . . the jailer,' said Clarity Jones. 'It, you know . . . it rhymes. Bayler the jailer.'

'**Ha! I get it!**' The guard gripping Clarity's left arm began to snigger. 'She's right – it does rhyme!'

'Oh yes –' Bayler snapped his stubby fingers together – 'Bayler . . . the jailer! Why have I never noticed that before?' He bent forward and gave a long, wheezing laugh.

'**Please help me . . . please! I'm going mad!**' screeched Horace from the next-door cell.

'Hehe, Bayler the jailer!' giggled the second guard, finally catching on.

'Well, that's made my day, that has.' Bayler dried his eyes with a thick knuckle before straightening up and clapping his hands together. 'Right, well – can't hang around here all day. We must get our new guest settled.'

He strode to the very end of the gloomy passageway and threw open the last door on the left. 'Here we are,' he announced. 'Room twelve. Best views in the house. In you go, then.' The guards half dragged Clarity to the door, one of them still chuckling, and flung her inside. She fell headlong on the hard floor, which was carved out of solid rock, and rolled over a few times before coming to a halt at the other edge of the cell. It was extremely lucky that she did stop at this point, because there was no wall. The back of the cell simply opened straight out on to the cliff, with what was admittedly a stunning view out to the west, where the sun was just beginning to set over the distant mountains.

'Told you there was a lovely view, didn't I?' said Bayler with no hint of irony. 'Now, do get yourself settled in. There's a lovely bed, and running water and everything. As I say, you'll be with us until you die, so do get as comfortable as you can. And if there's anything you need – anything at all – just let me know.'

'What, and you'll bring it to me?' asked Clarity, already suspecting what the answer was going to be.

'Oh no. No, no. But it keeps me amused.' And, with that, Bayler the jailer slammed the stout wooden door closed and retreated down the passageway with the guards, still laughing among themselves about his newly discovered rhyming name.

The dungeons' newest resident scrambled backwards in a sitting position from the cliff edge and looked about her. There was a rough ledge cut into one wall, which she assumed was meant to serve as her bed. A trickle of unwholesome-looking water was running down the centre of the floor along a narrow culvert that led from the door to out over the cliff edge. This, she realized, was the collected condensation from the damp passageway outside and was apparently what Bayler had meant by 'running water'. Clarity Jones, as we know, had been through many adventures in her life, and this, she decided, was by no means the worst situation she had ever found herself in. Gathering her long cloak about her to keep out the chill, she sat for a moment and thought. Bayler the jailer hadn't searched her before locking her away. He had assumed – correctly – that she had no weapons, as they'd all been left at the Strangers' Tower. But a good detective carries more than just weapons. And now she was no longer a princess, Clarity had many pockets to carry those things in.

Looking out across the city as the sun set, Clarity Jones began to make her escape plan. And, as she did so, she wondered whether the other members of her detective agency had realized the same thing she had: the Mystery of the Flying Fool was far, far more puzzling and dangerous than it had first appeared.

The Tale of Clarity Jones

Part III

A Dagger in the Dark

nce upon a time there was an assassin.

She grew up in the Assassins' Quarter of Meandermart, having been found on the streets as a very small orphan and taken in by the deadliest of the gangs, the White Hand Clan. From a young age she showed an incredible talent for climbing, jumping and hiding ~ three of the most useful talents for an up-and-coming assassin. And so, despite her tender age, the clan chiefs decided that she should be trained in their deadly ways. After all, she was rather small and very useful for sending in through narrow windows or secret tunnels.

The girl took to her assassin training like a whale to water. By the time she was seven, she could complete the secret assassin's training course across the rooftops of the city faster than any of her grown-up clan-mates. By the time she was ten, she was the sneakiest, the deadliest and the most sought-after assassin in the entire city.

Now it just so happened that, at about the same time, something rather unexpected had happened in the nearby Mages' Quarter. A mysterious woman named Clarity Jones had arrived in the city accompanied by a gigantic, warlike and very clean snow gnoblin from the mountains in the far south. Clarity, with Mirko now as a companion, had continued her journey, travelling back up the long road north from the kingdom of Informatia (which incidentally is called the Informatian Superhighway). She had finally settled on a job that would combine both her passions ~ discovering magic and solving mysteries ~ and had decided to set up shop as Meandermart's very first detective, a word that she had invented on her long journey.

And so she found a shop in a quiet, hidden corner of the Mages' Quarter. She wrote a sign in a very rare magic ink called electink ~ an ink that could only be seen by those who really, truly needed to see it, which would ensure nobody could find her shop in its shabby, forgotten square unless

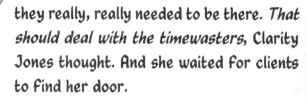

they really, really needed to be there. *That should deal with the timewasters,* Clarity Jones thought. And she waited for clients to find her door.

After a while her reputation began to spread. 'There's a woman in the Mages' Quarter,' people started whispering to each other, 'who can solve any mystery!' People with mysteries began to come looking for this intriguing person. And some of them ~ the ones that really, really needed to find her ~ discovered her shop in its tucked-away corner. And they paid her well to look into their problems. All well and good so far. But . . .

The problem was there were a lot of people in Meandermart who didn't want to have someone going around solving mysteries. They liked their mysteries to stay extremely mysterious. Take the assassins who plied their trade in the Assassins' Quarter, for instance. Their speciality was doing away with people in the dead of night and getting a lot of gold for doing so. They were silent; they were deadly; they left no trace behind. Until one day, when a certain merchant (who another merchant had taken a dislike to) ended up in the river, face down. And not just because he was going for a refreshing early-morning swim. Clarity Jones traced the assassin who'd, for want of a better word, assassinated him, and the City Watch came to arrest him.

Now, in this case, the assassin who'd been arrested didn't end up in prison. It was the four guards of the City Watch who ended up in the moat. The incident had been enough to attract the attention of a few very high-up people in the Assassins' Quarter. Notably, the leaders of the most powerful, sneakiest and deadliest of all the clans ~ the White Hand Clan. And the heads of the White Hand Clan sent their very best assassin to make sure that Clarity Jones wasn't going to solve any more mysteries. On account of having been assassinated. That's just the way they did stuff in that part of the city.

So one night, as Clarity Jones sat by candlelight in her detective shop, writing up her notes from her latest case, there was a slight breath of wind that made the candle in front of her gutter and flicker. And when she looked up, a small figure dressed from head to toe in black leather was standing in the centre of the room. She hadn't heard a thing ~ no door had creaked, no window had squeaked. That's not the way assassins work. They don't go around creaking and squeaking stuff. They're more in the 'silent, efficient killers' line of work.

But things that evening didn't work out quite as planned. Because instead of panicking and begging for her life, which most people would have done at this point, Clarity Jones simply reached down into a wooden chest that was dozing quietly at her feet and pulled out a small, round mirror. This startled the assassin girl slightly ~ people didn't generally stop to

do their hair before getting assassinated. She was more startled still when the woman got calmly up from her chair, her blue cloak billowing out behind her, and stood in the centre of the room with a vague smile.

'Come on, then,' the woman said, glancing down at the mirror in her hand.

Again, this was a surprising move. Most people did their best to avoid getting assassinated ~ it can really spoil your day. But here was this strange mystery-solving woman, literally standing up and presenting herself as an easy target! *Ah well*, thought the young assassin. *Don't look a gift tricorn in the horns.* And, pulling a slim dagger from her braided hair, she leaped forward.

At this point, Clarity Jones did the most unexpected thing yet. She dodged gracefully to one side, easily evading the attack. The assassin turned a rapid backwards somersault and came at her from a different angle, but once again the target moved aside at the last moment. This process went on for some time, with the assassin growing more and more frustrated. She was extremely good at her job and this had simply never happened before. Nobody had ever been able to predict her angle of attack like this woman was doing. Eventually, after ten minutes or so of thrusting and dodging, the girl stopped and put her hands on her hips.

'All right, all right,' said the assassin. 'How are you doing that?'

In reply, Clarity Jones held out the small mirror. In it, the assassin could see her own face, wearing an expression of amazement. 'It's a pre-flector,' the detective told her. 'It shows me what you're about to do.'

The assassin's face broke into an expression of amazement. 'That's the best thing I've ever seen,' she said, forgetting to be all cool and assassin-esque for a moment. 'What else have you got?'

'I'll show you,' said the detective with a smile, 'as long as you promise not to assassinate me in the meantime.'

In fact, by now the assassin had completely forgotten that that's what she'd come there to do. In all her years of training, she had never seen anything that fascinated her so much. And, if she was being honest with herself, she was really enjoying the atmosphere of this cosy room with its flickering fire and its gently dozing wooden chest on legs. It felt far more like home than the White Hand Clan headquarters, which were draughty and competitive and more than a little stabby.

Clarity Jones, meanwhile, had sensed a deep loneliness underneath the assassin's cold and efficient exterior. And she had also realized that her own job of being a detective had started to put her in a lot of danger. Having a top assassin on the team could be very useful indeed. She was looking at a massive win~win situation, basically, for all concerned, if she could

just persuade this deadly girl to join her agency.

'What's your name?' asked Clarity Jones. In reply, the assassin pulled a small business card from a pouch on her belt and held it out. 'This just says "assassin",' the detective said with a frown.

'You're reading it upside down,' the girl replied.

Clarity flipped the card over. 'Ah. Right. I see. Nissassa. How do you do? My name's Clarity Jones. I'm Meandermart's first-ever detective.'

'Hello,' replied Nissassa. 'What's a detective?'

CHAPTER 7

NEVER ELIMINATE
THE IMPOSSIBLE

Every year, the King of Rillia made a ceremonial visit to one of the main cities in his kingdom to commiserate the unfestive season of Moaningtide. It was the royal duty he disliked the most. At this time of the year, the roads were clogged with freezing, sticky mud that got stuck in the wheels of his state carriage. The eight tricorns that pulled the carriage got grumpy and uncooperative in the cold weather, and made this known by letting out complaining bleats all the way and spitting at bystanders. Meandermart was the most westerly city in Rillia, so the journey there was the longest, the muddiest, the bleatiest and the spittiest. Thus it came to pass that when, early one Moaningtide Eve, the king's carriage passed through the city's great east gate to the brassy sound of a trumpet fanfare, he was in a thoroughly bad mood. He could hardly have been any moodier – not even if he'd known that somebody in the city had hatched an extremely cunning and evil plan to attack him really quite violently during the next day's banquet . . . but we're getting ahead of ourselves.

King Bernard of Rillia was a kindly man but a sad one. Several years before, his family had been hit by a tragedy when his wife fell ill and died. Ever since then, the king had become quieter and more reserved, although he still carried out his duties as well as he could with the help of his sons. But there was something strained about his kingly smiles, something weak and unconvincing in his kingly handshakes and a twinkle missing from his previously bright and intelligent eyes. The people of Rillia never noticed this, of course. (It's rare for anyone to get close enough to a king to work out that he's wrestling with a secret sorrow; normally, you're too busy bowing and wondering what to say.)

And so that day, as he did every day, King Bernard of Rillia automatically carried out his duty, extending an arm out of the coach window to wave to the crowds as the bad-tempered tricorns pulled the carriage through the gates of Meandermart. Steam puffed from the trumpets on the ramparts as the heralds parped a welcome fanfare into the cold sky, and the assembled citizens gave a watery cheer as he passed by, clapping their chapped hands together and craning their cold red noses up to try to catch a glimpse of the royal personage. Despite the limp, unenthusiastic, circular wave that was offered to them, the Meandermartins were in an excited Moaningtide mood, looking forward to a whole day of complaining about the horrible winter weather. And so, as the barely waving king passed through the streets on his way to the castle, he was greeted with cheers, banners and the occasional friendly shout of 'It feels like it's never going to be summer again!' and 'I can't feel my toes!' and other traditional Moaningtide sayings of that ilk.

At one point along the route, a group of gripe singers had gathered, their breath visible in the chilly morning air, to serenade the royal visitor with one of his least-favourite unfestive tunes:

It's put-up-the-tree time.
It's such a beastly time.
It gets dark before teatime –
Oh folde-diddly oh, how I hate the winter.
Come hear me complaining.
It's cold and it's raining.
This is not entertaining –
Oh folde-diddly oh, how I hate the winter.

'"How I hate the winter",' sang King Bernard mournfully as he passed by the gripers. 'So true, so true,' he said to himself, nodding sadly. When he'd been a young man he had found Moaningtide rather depressing. These days, it had become his favourite holiday; a brief time of year when he didn't have to pretend to be cheerful. 'It really is the least wonderful time of the year,' he said to himself in glum satisfaction. Shivering, he pulled his hand back inside the carriage and swished the red velvet curtains closed, shutting himself off from the cold and the cheering Meandermartins outside.

One of the people who had gathered to watch the royal carriage pass through the streets was not cheering. He was thinking. Because Mutt had been thinking pretty much constantly since Nissassa had thrown him out of the Magical Detective Agency's shop the previous day. He had walked thoughtfully through the streets and thoughtfully bought a pie from the goat-pie man, who now greeted him like a long-lost cousin every time he saw him. He had thoughtfully taken the pie home, picking his way thoughtfully through Squelj and thoughtfully between the trees beside the river, and had sat thoughtfully on the wooden deck outside his empty house to eat the pie – thoughtfully – and stare thoughtfully at the sluggish, thick waters of the river as it slipped slowly past at the start of its long journey to the Great Sea.

There were so many things that didn't add up that it felt like a maths test in which the universe had scored nought out of ten. 'None of it makes sense, Mum,' Mutt said over his shoulder to one of the carved wooden lifna on the mantelpiece. 'I don't know what to do, Dad,' he said to the other. The figures looked out at him kindly. They were excellent listeners, as he'd discovered over the past few years.

'So, we rescued the jester,' he went on, deciding it might help if he told the story out loud to the wooden forms that commemorated his parents. 'But he wasn't in the least bit jesty. He was horrible, in fact. Not like everyone said he'd be. And he wasn't at all grateful to be rescued – he was really mean about it.' Mutt spun round to face into the room, dangling his legs over the edge of the hatch that led to the deck, and chewing meditatively on a deliciously seasoned chunk of goat pie. That secret blend of herbs and spices really was very good. 'And then,' Mutt continued, 'Ferdinand – who'd been so friendly – turned on us too! He turned traitor at the very moment we needed friendship.' The wooden eyes gazed at Mutt, reassuring but silent. 'You're right,' he replied. 'There must be a simple answer. Some detail that I'm missing . . .' But even though he pondered long and hard into the night as he lay beneath his (new, thicker) blanket, Mutt felt the answers slipping away from him before he could grasp them, like slender fish between his groping fingers.

Hours later, as dawn filtered through the long leaves outside his window, Mutt's legs carried him automatically out of bed and down to the riverbank to wash. Then, wrapped up warmly in his new clothes, he left the boat-house and headed towards the city. Wherever those answers were, he thought to himself, they weren't at home. And he wasn't going to find them by hanging about there, brooding. And so, when King Bernard passed by in his golden carriage, Mutt was standing among the crowd, still thinking like it was going out of fashion.

The bystanders began to disperse after the carriage had trundled away towards the Merchants' Quarter, but Mutt still remained there, deep in thought.

Several times people bumped into him and muttered angrily, jostling him out of the way as he stood motionless at the side of the street. He'd been knocked so many times, in fact, that it took him several minutes to register that something was nudging urgently at his left leg. Slowly, Mutt shook himself out of his reverie and looked down to find the source of this nudgery. There, planted on its hind legs and leaning up against him with the other two, was Clarity's wooden chest.

'**Smyll!**' said Mutt in surprise. 'Hello, boy. Where did you spring from?' The chest backed away a couple of steps and did a little dance to express its joy at being noticed. The bottles and boxes inside jingled as it capered. Normally, this would have attracted some attention – after all, it's not every day you see a wooden chest on legs dancing around in the street, not even in Meandermart – but by then the crowd that had turned out to greet the king had mostly gone, and the few hurrying figures still on the street were too wrapped up in their cloaks and their thoughts to pay much heed.

Smyll led Mutt along the street towards a small plaza. Some stubby trees had been planted, bare now in the mid-winter chill, and a few large stones were scattered about, where people could sit and take the air in the warmer months. Now, though, on this cold Moaningtide Eve, the square was deserted as Mutt, wrapping his cloak more tightly about himself, perched on a rock to try to work out why Clarity's chest of mystery-solving equipment had chosen to seek him out.

'What do you want, Smyll?' he queried, as the chest ran in circles in front of him. 'You want to know where your mistress is? She's locked in the castle dungeons, I'm afraid.' Smyll let out a small creak that sounded like a whine. 'But don't worry,' Mutt went on bracingly. 'Nissassa and Mirko will know what to do.' But even as he said the words, he realized they weren't true. The snow gnoblin had seemed just as flummoxed as he was, and Nissassa had been far too furious with Handy Dandy to think clearly.

With a funny little leap, the chest threw itself down on its tummy at Mutt's feet, flipping open its lid at the same time.

'What?' Mutt asked, confused. 'What are you trying to show me? I don't know what most of this stuff does yet – I've only been an assistant for, like, a week and a bit. Despite what Nissassa said, I'm still on trial. But I suppose that will have to finish now,' he added, the thought hitting him again like a sack of frozen chips to the gut.

Smyll gave another whine and jiggled. Mutt shook his head to clear away the mist of misery and tried to focus. What was the chest on legs trying to show him? Was there something among the phials and packets that might start to unlock this puzzle? He started sorting through the contents of the chest, picking out things at random. He examined a bottle marked, in Clarity's neat handwriting,

Lie Detonator

and a tub marked

Loca-Motive

and a box full of powder with a skull and crossbones carved into the top – he put this one back rapidly. As he did so, he noticed a small slip of paper tucked right in the back of the chest, near one of the hinges. Frowning, Mutt pulled it out and unfolded it. There, in that same small, sloping writing, were the words he'd heard Clarity Jones say so many times.

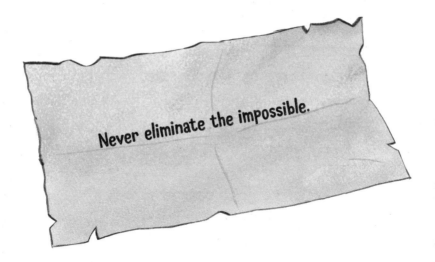

Never eliminate the impossible.

A sensible, grown-up voice inside Mutt's head was telling him that this was nothing unusual. Clarity had obviously written her motto down as a little reminder to herself, nothing more. And another, more miserable, voice was saying: *What's the point?*

What can a street dog do anyway? But Mutt ignored them both. Smyll the chest had tilted itself slightly, as if it was looking expectantly into his face. And, somewhere in his heart, he knew what the chest wanted to say to him: *Don't give up.* That's what Smyll had sought him out to say: *Don't lose hope. Look in unexpected places. We can solve this.*

'Thanks,' said Mutt, slamming the lid shut and rising to his feet with an air of determination. He clicked his fingers, just like Clarity, and the chest came obediently to heel, quivering with suppressed excitement.

'Come on, Smyll,' said Mutt, taking to his heels and breaking into a run. He began to head through the alleyways of Meandermart towards the Mages' Quarter. **'We've got a case to solve!'**

At the headquarters of the Magical Detective Agency, Mirko and Nissassa were barely speaking to each other. After an uneasy night's sleep and an even more uneasy 'good morning', they had retreated to opposite sides of the main room, each attempting to solve the mystery in a very different way. Mirko was back behind his desk, poring over an ever-growing stack of books and pages of notes, shaking his head every now and then as he looked in vain for some detail that he might have missed. Nissassa, on the other hand, was sitting at her usual table near the door, twirling her favourite dagger dexterously between the fingers of her left hand as she studied a large piece of parchment bearing a map of Meandermart Castle.

Now, it was illegal for anybody to have a map of the castle – its passageways and hallways were closely guarded secrets. But you don't get to be the city's top assassin without owning a few things you're not supposed to. And this map was one of the things Nissassa had saved when she'd left the chambers of the White Hand Clan, thinking – correctly, as it turned out – that it seemed like the sort of map that could well come in useful one of these days.

Nissassa's and Mirko's separate ponder-bubbles were both burst at exactly the same moment when Mutt crashed through the door, Smyll cantering obediently at his heels. **'NEVER ELIMINATE THE IMPOSSIBLE!'** he was yelling at the top of his voice.

Nissassa did what all assassins do when they're startled – she performed a backwards somersault off her chair and landed in a defensive crouch with no fewer than three separate daggers ready for action, one of them clutched in her teeth.

'It's me! It's me! Daggers down!' cried Mutt anxiously, holding his hands up, palms out in a gesture that would have been of no use whatsoever in an actual combat situation.

'What are *you* doing here?' snarled Nissassa, reluctantly sheathing her weapons. 'I told you yesterday, there's nothing more you can do.'

'Yes, there is,' replied Mutt stubbornly, jutting out his chin. 'I can help you solve the case.'

'*You?*'

'I'll ignore that sarcastic tone,' said Mutt graciously, 'because I know you're upset. But yes, me. Smyll came to me.' He gestured down towards the chest, which gave a small creak of agreement. 'Clarity trusted me. And so should you.'

There was a deep rumble from across the room and Mutt looked round in alarm. It sounded like an approaching stampede of something large with heavy feet. But after a second he realized with relief that it was simply the sound of Mirko breaking into a rolling laugh. The snow gnoblin stood up behind his desk, reaching up to wipe his eyes with a gigantic white furry paw. 'I always wondered when the finest assassin in Meandermart would meet her match,' he said, smiling. 'But I never thought she'd be bested by some grubby kid off the street.'

'**Hey,**' protested Mutt automatically. 'I'm not grubby any more.'

'You still don't wipe your feet properly,' grumbled Mirko, pointing to a puddle of muddy midwinter water that had collected at the hem of Mutt's cloak. 'But never mind that now. So . . . you've come to help us solve the case, have you? Well, Mr Great Detective, let's hear it. What's your big revelation?'

'**We've missed something blindingly obvious!**' said Mutt, coming to join Mirko at his desk. Nissassa gave a tut at this but he ignored her. 'We didn't follow Clarity's most essential piece of advice – in fact, she even forgot to follow it herself! We *eliminated the impossible.*' He started sorting through the piles of books on Mirko's desk. 'What was strange about Handy Dandy?' he said as he rifled through the stacks.

'Er, he was a complete and total pile of gnanger dung?' said Nissassa acidly, vaulting over her own desk and approaching with reluctant interest.

'Exactly!' said Mutt. 'And, before we met him, everybody said he was kind of annoying, but not horrible and insulting.'

'So?' Nissassa looked at him sceptically.

'So,' said Mutt with that air of slight smugness that is difficult to resist at moments like this, 'the person we rescued from that house – or, rather, the *creature* we rescued – wasn't Handy Dandy at all!' Triumphantly, he found the book he was looking for and leafed through the pages. After a moment he slammed it on to the desk and pointed.

Mirko leaned over him to see. It was the traveller's guide he'd been poring over a few days before, when they'd been trying to work out what could have flown away from the jester's window. 'A nyterra?' he said, sounding doubtful.

'Look,' said Mutt, 'it says here that nyterras are "legendary shapeshifting creatures". They're able to "assume the form of any other living creature". And,' he concluded with a satisfied nod, 'they can fly. Look.'

Nissassa was now also reading over his shoulder.

'But it can't be,' she said, as if explaining something to a child. 'It says right here – the last nyterra was killed more than ten years ago by a monster catcher. So there can't be a nyterra on the loose in Meandermart. It's . . .'

'Impossible?' Mutt turned to face the assassin. 'Right! That's what we all thought. So we moved on. But it's the only explanation that fits. And there's only one way to be sure.'

'Which is?' Mirko straightened up, his eyes lighting up with excitement. Suddenly, things didn't seem quite so hopeless.

Mutt headed for the door, Smyll bowling after him uttering a series of piercing, delighted yips. 'Follow me!' he told his team. 'We need to go and talk to Gabriel Ratchets the monster catcher.'

Back in the far-off days when the person now known as Clarity Jones had been a young princess, there had been many things she disliked about her position. She hated the fact that she was seldom allowed out of the castle. She hated the fact that everybody expected her to laugh politely and not say anything threateningly clever. She hated the fact that she was never allowed to ask questions about magic (which wasn't considered a proper pastime for royalty) or try to solve mysteries (which was already her dream job). But the thing she had hated most of all was this: no pockets. A princess was expected to swan about the place in gowns made of the finest materials, looking ethereal and floaty. And not a single one of these frilly, frothy frocks ever had a single pocket. So, after she gave up being a princess and set up as an adventurer and then, later, as Rillia's first-ever detective, Clarity Jones made sure that her outfits had a lot of pockets. Really, a lot. More pockets, some might say, than were strictly necessary.

As we know, Clarity Jones had an enchanted wooden chest named Smyll that followed her everywhere. And inside Smyll she kept most of her magical detecting equipment. But there were a few essential items that she liked to keep even more handy. Items that a detective might need in a hurry. And these she kept in some of her many pockets. Which is why, when dawn broke over Meandermart that morning, one of the prisoners in the deep dungeons set into the cliffs beneath the castle woke in a surprisingly good mood.

'**Morning! Breakfast time!**' fluted Bayler the jailer, pushing a rickety wooden cart down the passageway between the cells. 'Room service!' he added, pressing his face up to the bars of room twelve, the final cell on the left. 'What would you like? Scrambled eggs? Bacon roll? Nice hot cup of mulled whine?'

'I strongly suspect that you're not actually going to provide me with any of those things, Bayler,' replied Clarity Jones brightly from inside her cell. She was sitting calmly with her legs dangling over the cliff, watching the dawn light strike the faraway hills.

'Ooh, she's clever, this one,' said Bayler grudgingly, turning to dunk a wooden ladle into a large metal pot balanced precariously on the trolley. Grabbing a slice of very stale bread with his other hand, he dolloped a pat of steaming, brownish goo on the bread and Frisbee'd it neatly between the bars. It landed just behind Clarity with a wet *splat*. 'Stew on bread,' the jailer announced. 'That's what we're serving for breakfast today. Oh, and also for lunch.

And supper. Enjoy.' He reversed away, dragging the trolley behind him, to torment Horace a few cells down, the miserable wretch who had gone entirely mad after several years of constant stew on bread and fake politeness.

Clarity Jones reached behind her and plucked the stew on bread from the cell floor. It had landed stew-side down – doesn't it always? – so she had to scoop it from the ground. But she'd eaten far worse during her many adventures, and she knew she had to keep her strength up. She took a bite and chewed thoughtfully. With her other hand, she delved into a small pocket sewn into the inside of her belt, and pulled out a small piece of folded black cloth. *This ought to do it*, thought Clarity to herself. *This ought to do very nicely*. She just needed to pick the right moment.

CHAPTER 8

THE MONSTER CATCHER'S TALE

Gabriel Ratchets, Rillia's most famous monster catcher, lived in an old stone house right on the edge of the Truly Terrifying Forest. The trees came right up to the back wall of his house, which had no windows and was built of very, very thick stone. The monster catcher was an old man. Rarely was he ever seen inside the city walls. Instead, he spent most of his time alone with his memories, shut up inside his lonely house in the wilds. Sometimes travellers would seek him out and offer him money or treasures in return for him telling them his tales of beasts he'd tamed or slain. Every so often he was even invited to the castle to regale the lords and ladies there with a few stories about the dangerous battles or fantastic voyages he'd made when he was a young man. Never before, though, had anybody sought out the monster catcher with the sole purpose of accusing him of being a big fat liar. But there's a first time for everything.

Ratchets was sitting staring into the fire in the main room of his house. And, Reader, it's a room that's worth you taking a look at. So, before the Magical Detective Agents arrive and things get super awkward, let's take a minute to glance around, shall we? The high stone walls were almost completely covered with trophies from creatures the monster catcher had defeated in his youth. There were numerous sets of tricorn horns, some enormous claws that once belonged to a savage beast called a floofster (its name is deceptively cute), and a pair of fangs from the giant scuttle snake of the Western Hills. One wall was dominated by a gigantic skull with three eye sockets and only one nostril: the remains of a fire-spitting grotesk that had once menaced a town far to the south until the people had pooled all their money and sent messengers to beg

Gabriel Ratchets to come and help them. Beneath the grotesk skull was a fireplace deep and wide enough for a person to stand up in – even a person as large as the monster catcher himself. And he was large – even now, as an old man, his shoulders bulged beneath the thick blanket he had wrapped round himself as he sat in his comfortable chair and gazed at the flames, his head full of memories of his past triumphs.

After a while, the old man lifted his head and listened. His large ears had spent a lifetime listening for approaching danger, and even though those ears were now covered by hair that was thin and white instead of lustrous and golden, they were still finely tuned. The monster catcher frowned to himself. Someone was coming. No, not just someone. He tilted his head on one side and leaned forward in his chair. One . . . two . . . three people. One of them large. And something else. Little skittering footsteps on the rocky path that led up to his front door and on into the forest. Three visitors, then, and a dog of some kind. He groaned, his knees clicking as he pushed himself out of his chair and laboured to his feet. More people come to hear his stories of long ago, no doubt, looking for some tales to take back to their Moaningtide feast. Ah well. Best put on a show for them. He walked stiffly to a large cupboard set into one wall, opened it and took out his monster-catcher hat. Visitors always seemed to love the hat.

Mirko stepped forward and knocked firmly on the stout wooden door before stepping back to join the others, rubbing his paws together against the cold.

'I can't wait to find out what this old fraud's got to say for himself,' said Nissassa grimly. 'If it turns out he lied about the last nyterra, and it's put Clarity in danger . . .' She left the rest of the sentence hanging ominously in the chilly mist that seemed to flow out from the closely packed trees behind the house.

'Leave the talking to me, all right?' said Mutt pleadingly. 'He's never going to tell us the truth if you barge in there and start being all assassin-y.'

'Fine,' grumbled Nissassa. 'All yours, Mr Detective. But, if you don't get some answers out of him, it's dagger time.' She pointed significantly to the hilt of her favourite dagger, which Mutt suddenly remembered was named Genevieve, protruding from a hidden sheath beneath her left arm.

'Oh, I think I'll get some answers all right,' said Mutt, hoping to himself that his idea would pay off. After all, he had no clue how this stuff was supposed to work. But it was worth a try. His musings were interrupted by a rattling noise, a thunk and then a loud creak as the door of the cottage was thrown open. And there, silhouetted in the opening, was a broad, hulking figure with antlers towering over its head.

'Welcome, travellers,' boomed a deep voice from the imposing creature in the doorway. 'Prepare yourselves to be terrified, mystified and –' He broke off into a rattling cough. 'Sorry . . . And, erm, terrified!'

'You've said "terrified" already,' Nissassa pointed out acidly.

'By tales of frightening beasts, horrifying monsters and scary – sorry –' The figure coughed again, bending down and placing his hands on his knees so the antlers poked out of the doorway, causing the visitors to take a step back. ' . . . And scary, ahem, scary animals.'

'That's just three ways of saying exactly the same

thing,' pointed out Nissassa.

'Well, if you've just come to pick holes in everything I say,' said the monster catcher, straightening up and looking at her crossly, 'why bother trekking all this way out of town to come and see me, huh?' He came out of the doorway slightly, and the light fell on his face. It was lined with deep wrinkles and heavily tanned, and the hair tumbling out from beneath the antler hat was snow-white, but Mutt could see the handsome man he must once have been.

'We've come to ask you some questions, if it's not too much trouble,' he said politely. 'My name's Mutt, and this is Mirko and this is Nissassa. We're detectives.'

'What?' The monster catcher took yet another step forward, peering at them closely. 'I've heard a lot of strange words in my time, young master, but that's a new one. And a snow gnoblin, eh?' Mirko gave a shallow, polite bow. 'Spent some time among your people a-ways back,' Ratchets went on. 'We went out into the blizzard forests hunting for slaughs. Good eating. And who have we here? An assassin.' He narrowed his eyes as he turned his head to take in Nissassa's black clothes and dagger-decorated hair braid.

'Retired assassin,' she corrected him automatically.

'Retired or not, I don't want no quarrels with your kind,' said Ratchets suspiciously.

'Then I strongly suggest you don't give me a reason to quarrel with you,' she replied calmly, pulling out a small, stout knife from the crook of her elbow, tossing it into the air and catching it behind her back.

'We come in peace!' said Mutt, shushing her with his left hand. His scheme wouldn't work unless they got the old man talking. If he shut the door in their face, they'd never find out what they needed to know. 'If we could please just come in for a few minutes,' he pleaded. 'We mean you no harm, and our friend is in terrible danger!'

Gabriel Ratchets eyed him curiously for a moment, then gave a curt nod and disappeared back into his house. As they entered, Mutt paused to read a painted wooden sign beside the front door.

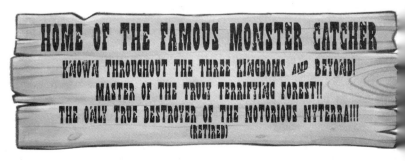

HOME OF THE FAMOUS MONSTER CATCHER
KNOWN THROUGHOUT THE THREE KINGDOMS AND BEYOND!
MASTER OF THE TRULY TERRIFYING FOREST!!
THE ONLY TRUE DESTROYER OF THE NOTORIOUS NYTERRA!!!
(RETIRED)

As he ushered the detectives into the woodsmoke-scented room, the monster catcher removed his antler hat and tossed it on to a chair. 'Waste of time getting that out,' he muttered as he crossed back to his fireside seat. 'Usually they love the hat. Go mad for the hat, they do. I don't know . . . kids these days.' He threw himself back into his armchair, tutting.

The members of the Magical Detective Agency, meanwhile, fanned out in front of the chair. Mutt reached down and gave a gentle click of his fingers, summoning Smyll to his side. The wooden chest obediently came to heel, kneeling down and flipping its lid open. 'That's something I've never seen before,' said Ratchets, leaning forward again. 'That's some neat magic, that. You don't see the likes of that these days.'

'Isn't it clever?' said Mutt in a friendly tone. 'Come on, Smyll, come over here with me and let this gentleman have a look at you.' He led the chest, still with its lid open, towards the armchair. 'He's a very, very famous man,' Mutt told Smyll. 'A great monster catcher. Finest in the whole kingdom. People tell amazing tales about his bravery all the time.'

A smile broke out on Ratchets' wizened face. 'What you got in there then?'

Mutt pulled a couple of boxes and jars out of the chest. 'All kinds of magical things,' he explained. 'My friend spent years and years putting this together. She travelled all across the Three Kingdoms and beyond. You two would have a lot to talk about. Oh, sorry!' Mutt had just been showing the old man a small red phial when he fumbled it. The stopper came away from the bottle and the liquid spilled out into the air, immediately turning into a crimson gas that coiled round the two of them with a strange crackling sound.

'Gargh! What's that stuff?' Gabriel Ratchets coughed and fanned a hand in front of his face.

'Oh, sorry – clumsy me! It's nothing dangerous. Don't worry.' Mutt put the empty bottle back in the chest and took a step backwards. 'Now, Mr Ratchets, we don't want to keep you long, but we really, really want to hear a tale about your monster-catching days, if it's not too much trouble.'

'Ah, you do, do you? And what was you wanting to know?' Ratchets sat back with a suspicious glance down at Smyll.

'Well, if it's not too much trouble –' Mutt smiled encouragingly – 'we really want to ask about the last nyterra.' At this, the old man burst into another fit of coughing. 'I was reading that it was a really, really terrifying beast,' Mutt went on. 'It must have been one of your greatest-ever triumphs, ridding the world of such a monster. We'd love to know how you did it.'

A glimmer came into the old man's eyes as he looked inwards, towards the past. 'Ah yes, the nyterra,' he said softly. 'Proper frightening, they was. The kingdom's well rid of them.' He paused for a moment in thought. 'And that's all you wants to know?' he asked, raising a thick white eyebrow.

'That's it,' said Mutt. 'Tell us what happened and we'll go.'

And Gabriel Ratchets the monster catcher told them the following story:

Once, long ago, deep in the darkest, most dangerous forest in all of Rillia, there lived a flock of creatures straight out of a nightmare. Nyterras were few, but terrifying nonetheless. They

haunted the most isolated, loneliest part
of the wood, living there for hundreds
of years in solitude and malice.

('This is all very atmospheric,' said Nissassa testily,
'but is there any chance of hurrying it up a bit? We're
kind of on the sundial here.' This is what Rillians say
instead of 'on the clock', because there aren't clocks
in Rillia. Gabriel Ratchets frowned at her and carried
on with his story.)

Nyterras were rare creatures with a
magical power that struck fear into
the hearts of all but the very bravest.
For once a nyterra had spent a day or
two observing another living being, it
was able to morph itself into an exact
replica of that creature, whatever it
might be. Mostly these beasts spent
their time in the forest, alone. But

every so often one of them would decide to go hunting among the world of humans. And when they did, they would always capture someone and bring them back to their lair in the forest. Then, after a while, the nyterra would assume their captive's form and go back to the town where they lived.

The townsfolk would wonder what had happened, because although the nyterra would look and sound exactly like the person they knew, the creature couldn't stop its true nature from showing through. And its true nature was pure evil. Nyterras lived only to torment and frighten.

(Mutt interrupted the old man's story at this point. 'And what about the real person?' he said. 'Once the nyterra had copied them, what happened? Did they die?'

Ratchets chuckled. 'No, they didn't die, young master. No. They fell into a deep sleep, and the nyterra would hide them away somewhere safe. Then, later, when the creature took on a new form, the captive would awake with no idea what had happened to them.'

Mutt furrowed his brow in thought as the story continued.)

Once people realized what was going on, they decided to rid the world of this menace once and for all. One by one, the nyterras were hunted down and killed. And I'm sorry to say, more than one innocent person was also hunted down, just because they had been mean or grumpy one day and their friends thought they'd been copied. But, eventually, only one nyterra was left in the whole of Rillia. It was known to have its lair deep, deep in the heart of the Truly

Terrifying Forest. And the citizens of Meandermart paid all the gold they could afford to the one person who could track it and finish it off. Because not far from their city lived a great monster catcher. And he was willing to take on the job. The legendary Hunt for the Last Nyterra had begun. The monster catcher took his sword, he took his bow and arrows, and he plunged deep into the woods. He finished off quite a few squirrels, because they looked kind of mean and he thought they might actually be the nyterra, but it turned out they were just mean squirrels. Good eating, though.

('Yuck,' muttered Nissassa.)

But eventually, in the dark heart of the Truly Terrifying Forest, the monster catcher came upon the beast's lair. The nyterra was in its true form, as black and leathery as a giant bat, with claws like a huge lizard and the face of some hideous bird. The nyterra leaped at the intrepid monster catcher, snatching his bow before he could shoot, and a great battle was joined.

(And, at this point, Gabriel Ratchets pulled his long white hair aside to reveal a long, angry scar just in front of his right ear before carrying on with his tale.)

Long they fought, man and beast. Through the trees the monster catcher chased his prey as it tried to flee. Finally, he ran it to ground, wounded and tired, in a glade near

the forest's edge. And there he plunged his sword deep into the creature's chest. The last nyterra was ... finally ... dead. Aaaaaaaaaa-CHOO!

BANG!

Mirko and Nissassa took a step back as the monster catcher's tale took a slightly unexpected turn. Because, as soon as he had said the word 'dead' he let out a huge sneeze, which came out as a puff of red smoke, and this smoke then exploded right in his face with a crack like a firework. Mutt, however, didn't look surprised. He simply smiled and said, 'I wonder whether you want to try that part of the story again, Mr Ratchets?'

Gabriel Ratchets looked at him with an expression that mingled confusion and fury. **'What have you done?'** he demanded angrily.

'The substance in that bottle is called "lie detonator",' Mutt explained. 'I wasn't quite sure how it would work, but I think we just found out. And we also discovered something very interesting, which is this: you didn't kill the last nyterra at all, did you?'

'I did!' insisted the monster catcher, before letting out another huge sneeze.

BANG!

This one, too, blew up in his face.

'I ran it through with my sword!' he said cautiously. No sneeze.

'Clearly that's true,' said Mutt. 'But it didn't die, did it?'

Ratchets looked as if he was about to insist once again that the nyterra had been killed, but thought better of it. 'All right then,' he muttered, looking crestfallen. 'Yes, all right, young master. I suppose the truth was bound to catch up with me sooner or later. It wasn't dead. I thought it was, though, truly I did!' He raised his voice pleadingly. 'I dragged it to the edge of the forest and people came to see. They lifted me on their shoulders and carried me back to the city. They showered me with gold! There were banquets, and they wrote songs about me. I knew I should have made quite sure it was dead, but . . .'

'But you were too busy being celebrated and

getting rich telling everyone your stories,' finished Nissassa for him, looking icy.

'So, what did happen to the nyterra?' asked Mirko urgently.

'I don't know,' said Ratchets in a high-pitched tone, before adding another '**Aaaa-CHOO!**'

BANG!

'All right, all right. I heard the beastmaster took it,' he finally admitted. 'Always looking for strange creatures for the shop, is the beastmaster.'

'I know that shop,' said Mutt to the others. 'Come on, there's no time to lose! We've got to find out what happened next.' Mutt and Nissassa and Mirko and Smyll all ran for the door and disappeared out into the cold afternoon.

'Oi!' Ratchets shouted after them. 'How long does this stuff last? I mean, I don't tell many lies . . . **Aaaaa-CHOO!**'

They heard the loud **BANG!** echoing through the forest as they ran back towards the city gate.

'It's this way,' panted Mutt half an hour later, leading the others through the Merchants' Quarter. Sure enough, tucked away in a side street was a grimy house with bars across the windows. The word

BEASTMASTER

was painted above the door, and a sign beside it read:

DEALER IN FANTASTICAL BEASTS, MONSTERS.
PETS FOR THE CHILDREN!
BODY PARTS AVAILABLE FOR MAGE WORK.
GOLD PAID FOR CAPTURED CREATURES.

Mirko hammered on the door.

'All right, all right, I'm coming,' said a quavering voice from inside.

After a few moments, the door opened to reveal an old woman looking up at them suspiciously. Mutt realized at once that he'd seen her before, but couldn't immediately remember where.

'Oh, it's you lot,' said the old lady, pulling the door all the way open. 'Have you finally decided to help me find Tiddles?'

CHAPTER 9

RIDDLES AND TIDDLES

'Come in, come in, out of the cold. You'll catch your deaths out there.'

The Beastmaster of Meandermart fussily ushered the Magical Detective Agents into her shop. 'Don't get close to the cages, will you?' she warned them as she shut the door behind them and bustled over. Two walls of the large room were lined with wooden cages that went from floor to ceiling. Mutt leaned forward to read a few of the labels. He saw that one cage held something called a peeky pooka (two eyes peered at him from a nest of straw right at the back). Beneath the peeky pooka's cage was a large tank with a glass top. Mutt jumped as a slimy tentacle broke the surface of the water.

'Noctapus,' the old lady told him. 'Nine legs. Very rare, that. Got it off a fisherman.'

'You're the woman who kept asking us to look for her lost cat!' Nissassa burst out.

'That's right,' said the old lady. 'I wish you'd helped me. Ran off, he did, and he'd been acting so strangely. Then, later, I found him, all curled up in the cellar.'

'Fast asleep?' said Mutt. 'Then, later, did he wake up and was he back to his old self?'

'That's right!' The beastmaster looked surprised. 'You seem to know a lot about Tiddles.' At that point, a large ginger cat stalked into the room and began to wind itself round Nissassa's legs, purring loudly.

'Why do they always pick me out?' she said moodily. 'I don't even like cats.'

'Where's the nyterra?' asked Mutt, deciding they'd beaten about the bush for long enough.

'What?' The old lady's face drained of colour and she sank back on to a stool.

'I said, where's the nyterra?' Mutt repeated. 'Or where *was* it, at least? The monster catcher's told us everything. We know you took it after his battle. And we know it wasn't quite dead.'

'I don't know what you're talking about,' said the beastmaster. Mirko took a threatening step forward, but Mutt held up a hand to stall him.

'How about this?' he suggested. 'I'll give you some theories, and you tell me if I'm right. Agreed?'

She gave a shaky nod.

'You kept it in the cellar, right?' he asked.

Her eyes widened. 'How could you know that?' she asked.

'Because that's where you found Tiddles,' Mutt told her. 'The nyterra had copied your cat. I suppose it had finally recovered its strength after all these years, and when it saw Tiddles wandering around the shop it decided to copy him.'

'Well,' said the beastmaster, holding her hands up in defeat, 'you seem to know most of it, so I might as well tell you the rest. You're right – I did take that nyterra thing. I've always been fascinated by strange animals, and I thought some of the parts might be useful to sell on to mages and the like. But, when I got it back here, I realized that that stupid monster catcher hadn't quite finished it off. So I put it down in the cellar, and told it I'd keep it safe. I'd throw it something to eat every now and then. But, for years and years, it did nothing. Then, all of a sudden, Tiddles started acting differently.'

'Let me guess,' said Mutt. 'Kind of evil?'

'Kept scratching me,' said the beastmaster. 'Then just vanished one day, he did – him what's never run off before and all!'

'I think we've learned just about all we need to know, thank you,' said Mutt. 'Just one more thing. Do you know Underduke Ferdinand?' He heard Mirko and Nissassa gasp behind him.

'Oh yes!' The beastmaster's wrinkled old face brightened up. 'Ever such a nice young man, he is. Always coming in for a chat. Always fascinated by strange creatures, he is. Loves the dangerous ones. Oh yes, I know Underduke Ferdinand.'

The Moaningtide commiserations were building to a climax. In the castle, King Bernard was being serenaded with a festive pageant depicting all the most miserable things about winter, while a band of minstrels played a selection of seasonal songs including 'I Just Can't Seem to Get Properly Dry' and 'The Tips of My Ears, They Hurt So Bad'. Duchess Peruka sat beside him, and next to her the jester Handy Dandy was watching her closely, his eyes burning with a strange light.

Meanwhile, throughout the city of Meandermart, people made their final preparations for the great feast that would be held the following day, marking the very centre point of winter and the most horrible, dark, cold, unpleasant moment of the entire year. The streets were full of the sound of gripe singers and the smell of cooking.

One place where nobody was preparing for a feast was the small shop in the Mages' Quarter where the members of the Magical Detective Agency had gathered after their clue-finding frenzy of a day. There's no time to plan a banquet when you've got a rescue to arrange.

'Just run me through it one more time,' Nissassa asked Mutt, still looking slightly needled that she hadn't worked it all out for herself.

'Underduke Ferdinand wants to stage an attack on the king,' repeated Mutt, 'and he wants to make it look like it's his sister, the duchess, doing it.

Ferdinand must have discovered the nyterra on one of his visits to the beastmaster's shop and worked out what it was. Somehow he convinced it to help him. So, first of all, the nyterra copied Tiddles the cat and Ferdinand took it to the castle. But the duchess didn't like the cat because it was mean and kept scratching her. So Ferdinand knew he had to try something different. He needed something – or somebody – who would be close enough to his sister for long enough to copy her. The nyterra needs days to do that, remember.'

'So he decided on her jester!' Mirko took up the story. 'The nyterra, disguised as Tiddles the cat, followed Handy Dandy to his room. It took on its true form, picked the jester up in its beak and flew out of the window with him.'

'And, at that point, the real Tiddles woke up,' added Mutt.

'And so the nyterra then learned to copy Handy Dandy, and we ended up taking this evil creature right back into the castle, thinking we were rescuing a stupid jester!' said Nissassa sulkily. 'Great. And that complete cess-hole Ferdinand used the opportunity to get Clarity out of the way, because he'd seen her at work and was worried she'd figure out what was really going on. *Grrr*, he's just risen to the top of my assassination list.'

'What we need to do urgently is warn the duchess about this,' said Mirko. 'If the shapeshifting nyterra copies her and attacks the king, she'll be executed.'

'That's exactly what Ferdinand's counting on!' realized Nissassa. 'That sneaky little . . .' She left the words hanging in the air for a moment. 'He'll get to be Warden of Meandermart!'

'So . . . how do we warn the duchess?' said Mutt seriously. 'And how do we convince her we're telling the truth?'

'We need to show her the real Handy Dandy,' said Mirko. 'There's no way anybody could argue with that! He must still be in that house in the Merchants' Quarter. And, all the while the nyterra's in the castle mimicking him, he'll be fast asleep!'

'Right.' Nissassa got to her feet. 'Here's the plan. We track down the real Handy Dandy. Somehow we get him into the castle, even though we're not allowed anywhere near it. We show him to the duchess and Clarity gets released.'

'I can see a few slight problems with that plan,' said Mutt in a worried tone. 'Like, didn't you say it's impossible to break into Meandermart Castle?'

'I certainly did,' said Nissassa with a smile that looked as sharp as one of her daggers. 'But, remember, street dog?' And here she looked Mutt full in the face and, for the first time, favoured him with a real smile, albeit a slightly wolfish one (but, hey, that's the only kind assassins can really do convincingly).

'We never eliminate the impossible!' shouted

Mutt and Nissassa at the same time, as he returned her smile with a less wolfish one of his own.

'I actually reminded you of that motto earlier today,' Mutt pointed out.

'All right, all right.' Nissassa patted him on the shoulder. 'Don't get too full of yourself. Now – let's go and get that unconscious jester!'

And with this slightly unconventional catchphrase, the Magical Detective Agents embarked on a new phase of their strangest and most dangerous case yet.

Elbric Smear does not feature heavily in this story. In fact, he's only in two scenes, so it's not worth getting to know him particularly well. But let's take a quick look at him anyway, because Mirko's going to knock him out cold in about seventeen paragraphs' time, so this will be our last chance.

Smear was a merchant. He owned the very fine old house built right on the city walls where Handy Dandy – or rather, as we now know, the nyterra pretending to be Handy Dandy – had been tied up in a chair, rather conveniently situated right in the middle of the front room. This, of course, had all been part of Underduke Ferdinand's dastardly plan – a plan he had paid Elbric Smear an eye-wateringly gigantic amount of gold to help him out with.

Underduke Ferdinand really had to congratulate himself on the genius of his plan. When the cat hadn't worked out, he'd been at a loss. Then it had hit him. The jester! Of course! Handy Dandy was always hanging around his sister – the perfect candidate for replacement by the nyterra. There had been a slight setback when that detective had been worryingly perceptive, but that was the point at which Ferdinand had yet another genius idea. Blame the detective for everything! She'd be out of the way, and the nyterra would be free to prepare for his masterstroke – the moment when Ferdinand's sister would apparently attack the king right in the middle of the Moaningtide banquet. His sister would be executed, and he'd be a hero and live happily ever after. He'd always wanted to do that.

So, anyway, back to Smear. The merchant had been instructed by Ferdinand to leave his front door unlocked on a particular night – the night Handy Dandy disappeared from the castle. He was also to leave the hatch that led to his cellar open, and go to bed. Under no circumstances was he to come out of his bedroom until morning. So Smear had nestled underneath his very thick and expensive blankets, listening with his very thick and expensive brain to the thuds, squeals and grunts as the nyterra wrestled Handy Dandy inside the house and pulled him down into the cellar. Ferdinand had then bolted the hatch shut, and waited. When the creature was ready and had assumed the jester's form, Ferdinand brought him up from the cellar and tied him to the chair in the middle of the front room, all ready for the Magical Detective Agents to affect their daring rescue. Ferdinand left the real Handy Dandy down in the cellar, in a deep, unconscious sleep.

It was Elbric Smear's job now to keep an eye on the sleeping jester in his cellar. But something was making him nervous. Something at the back of his mind kept telling him that, once the underduke had become the actual duke, he wasn't going to trust Smear to keep quiet about his part in the plot. He was starting to suspect that, one dark night, he'd find an assassin in his house. Or, rather, *he* wouldn't find one. An assassin would find *him*. And the first thing he'd know about it was when he'd wake up and discover that he'd been assassinated in his sleep. Which can really put a dampener on anybody's morning. So, at this point in the tale, Smear was pacing anxiously up and down his front room, rubbing his hands together nervously and giving some really serious thought to moving his mercantile operations to a completely different city. Possibly throwing in a change of name and a different appearance for good measure.

'Some kind of large hat, possibly,' he was muttering as he formed his plans. 'A floppy one. And perhaps a beard! Yes! A beard! That would be –
AAAAAARGGGGGH!'

The reason Elbric Smear had finished this sentence in quite such a dramatic fashion was not that he suffered from an extreme fear of beards. It was because, for the second time that week, the stout double doors at the front of his house had been smashed off their hinges by Mirko. Framed in the doorway were three figures: the central one huge and shaggy, the one on the left a child of some description, and the one on the right . . . well, she could only be an assassin.

Smear panicked! They'd come for him already! Gibbering, he attempted to back away rapidly into his house but tripped over and instead ended up pushing himself along backwards by his heels, his shoulders scraping along the floor as he uttered a series of terrified squeaks.

'What on earth do you think you're doing?' roared the shaggy shape in the doorway. Mirko marched over to the moaning merchant and, reaching down and plucking the merchant's velvet jacket between two of his claws, lifted him clear into the air. 'Where's the jester?' asked the snow gnoblin in a friendly tone.

'A-bah, a-bah, a-bah, a-bah, woot, hemmm?' replied Smear, which was no help whatsoever. His legs bicycled frantically as Mirko held him up higher and gave him a slight shake.

'Don't want to talk, huh?' snarled Nissassa, vaulting over to examine him.

'I don't think he *can* talk right now,' corrected Mutt, following her. 'He's completely terrified – look.'

'Hmmmm.' Nissassa peered into the merchant's face. 'I wonder what's got this little creep so spooked.'

'I don't know anything about it!' squeaked Smear suddenly.

'I'm not altogether sure I believe you.' She reached for her belt. 'How about I start cutting off parts of you until you remember something useful?'

'The jester is in the cellar,' gabbled Smear. 'The trapdoor is in that room over there.'

'That's better.' With an unnecessary but very cool handspring, Nissassa leaped through a doorway, and Mutt heard the creaking of rusty bolts as she opened the cellar hatch and jumped down. 'He's here!' she said after a moment. 'Fast asleep, just like the street dog said!' ('Oi!' said Mutt.)

'Thanks so much for your help,' said Mirko politely to Elbric Smear, before bunching one of his huge hands into a fist and hitting the merchant squarely on the head with it. Smear immediately began to snore loudly, and as Nissassa reappeared, dragging the real Handy Dandy by his arms, Mirko placed Smear neatly in a large armchair by the fire and turned to face the rest of the team. 'Right,' he said in a satisfied tone. 'We've got the unconscious jester.'

'Best kind, if you ask me,' added Nissassa.

'Now all we need to do is get inside the heavily

defended and previously impenetrable Meandermart Castle, which everyone agrees is completely impossible,' said Mirko.

'Meh,' said Nissassa. 'People are always saying that stuff's impossible. They only say that because nobody's ever actually done it before. Once you do it, it's no longer impossible. Piece of cake.'

'You sound like you might have a plan,' said Mutt hopefully.

'I do have a plan,' said Nissassa. 'But –' and here she looked at Mirko – 'we're going to need a distraction.'

CHAPTER 10

A DISTRACTION

It was just before dawn on Moaningtide Day, the very darkest, the very coldest, the very dankest, most miserable, depressing, horrible part of the whole long winter. A freezing fog lay draped across the city of Meandermart, sending icy fingers trailing across the dark houses. Deep inside the castle, sleepy servants gave face-cracking yawns as they lit the first fires to start preparing for the great banquet to be held later that day. And outside on the long sloping causeway that led up to the main gates, guards stamped and rubbed their numb hands together as they kept watch. This early-morning duty was the most dismal of all – the one the castle guards tried their hardest to avoid. The ones who were unlucky enough to be standing out in the freezing cold that dark Moaningtide morn were cursing their ill luck, not realizing that they were about to experience something stupendous. Something that had never been seen in this part of the world before. They were about to gain a story that they would go on to bore their families with every single Moaningtide Day from then on. And many of them were about to get really quite badly hurt in the process. Because the members of the Magical Detective Agency were about to do what nobody had ever done before – break into Meandermart Castle.

'We're going to need some proper hardware for this one,' Nissassa had declared as they marched back into the agency's headquarters.

'You seem to have quite a lot of hardware already,' said Mutt doubtfully, eyeing the dagger hilts that studded her braided hair, and thinking too of the countless other weapons that he knew were secreted in a bewildering variety of hiding spots about her person.

'Oh, this is just for every day,' she told him. She strode over to one of the large bookcases that lined the wall behind her desk. 'Storming the castle is more of a special occasion.' And, with that, she pulled forward on one of the thick books that lined the middle shelf. It was, Mutt could see, entitled *The Floomfy Baby Kitten Companion*. 'Clarity chose the book,' explained the retired assassin. 'I think she was teasing me.' With a *clank*, the bookcase shifted slightly outwards towards them before sliding smoothly to one side with a barely audible whirring and ticking of hidden but evidently extremely well-oiled machinery. Behind it was a smallish room lined from floor to ceiling with rack upon rack of weaponry and equipment. The firelight from the main chamber shone on polished blades, pieces of protective armour and strange polished gadgets of all kinds.

'*Retired* assassin, huh?' questioned Mutt, casting his eye over the startling array of hardware.

'Well . . . possibly semi-retired,' she conceded, 'for today, at least. Right.' Hands on hips, she stood in the entrance to the weapon-lined room and considered. 'Who shall I take? You, for certain, Florence.' She plucked a short, fat-bladed sword in a soft black scabbard from the wall and placed it at her feet. 'And you two can definitely come along, Bernice and Margery.' Two long-bladed daggers were added to the pile. 'Don't be sad, Genevieve,' called Nissassa over her shoulder. Mutt half turned to see that her favourite dagger, its black hilt studded with gleaming onyx gemstones, was lying on her desk by the door. 'You won't miss out. You'll all get to share in the fun, I promise.'

'Do you get the impression,' asked Mirko in an undertone, bending down to talk close to Mutt's ear, 'that she spent her childhood playing with swords and daggers the way most kids play with toys?' Mutt stifled a short laugh as Nissassa continued adding to the pile of equipment at her feet, selecting a coil of soft, slim black rope and a pair of thick leather gloves embroidered with what appeared to be cats' faces in delicate purple thread.

'So, this distraction . . .' said Mutt to Mirko.

'Ah yes,' said the huge snow gnoblin, smoothing his white fur meditatively. 'The distraction. That's going to be my job. Yes, hang on a moment . . .' And, with that, he vanished through a door at the side of the room. Clanking, banging and the screeching sound of metal rubbing against metal floated back through the door, making Mutt clench his teeth. 'It'll be quite the distraction, I promise you!' came the snow gnoblin's voice along with the noise. 'This is something nobody in Meandermart has ever seen, apart from that monster catcher . . . Only brought this stuff with me in case of a real emergency – and I'm fairly sure this qualifies.'

'Erm, yes . . . Do you mean the plot we've uncovered to attack the king and get the duchess executed? The plot to take over Meandermart using a hugely dangerous and terrifying monster?' queried Mutt. 'Yes, I think we can definitely classify that as an emergency.'

'Exactly.' The clanking and banging continued.

'So what's this distraction then?' asked Mutt.

'Well, it's nothing very complicated, really,' said Mirko, to the accompaniment of more metallic clangs. 'I'll simply walk up to the main gates and keep all the guards busy, while you and Nissassa sneak up the cliffs with Handy Dandy.'

'Wait – what?' Mutt sank down on to a stool, feeling like all his hopes were leaking out through his heels. 'Keep *all* the guards busy? Do you know how many guards there are in Meandermart Castle?'

'Do you?' retorted Nissassa.

'Well . . . no,' he admitted. 'But I'm betting it's a lot. And *climb the cliffs*?' His voice broke with disbelief. 'That's crazy! The cliffs at the back of the castle can't be climbed!' In his years of pounding the city streets, he'd seen those cliffs every day, rising sheer from the Oxbow Moat at the back of the castle, grey and jagged and very, very unclimbable-looking.

'You're just saying that because nobody has ever climbed them,' pointed out Nissassa. 'I'm pretty sure I can get us up, once the guards are out of the way. Usually there are archers stationed at the top to pick off anyone climbing, but once they see Mirko they'll call all the guards to the front gate – I'm certain of that. They'll never have seen anything like it before!'

'Can't we just, you know, walk up to the front gate with the real Handy Dandy and show him to the guards?' asked Mutt, wondering why nobody had thought of this rather simple solution before.

'The duchess ordered the guards to shoot us on sight if we ever go near the castle, remember?' Nissassa told him. 'You'd be stuck full of arrows like a little hedge-hawk before you got close enough to show them the jester. You don't want to be stuck full of arrows, do you?'

Mutt agreed that he didn't, but then held up a hand. 'Wait a minute, though,' he said. Nissassa broke off from her equipment-gathering to pay attention to him. She looked at him curiously, her head cocked to one side. 'If the castle guards have orders to shoot us on sight,' continued Mutt, 'then how is Mirko going to march up to the gates and distract them all? And what did you mean by "they'll never have seen anything like it before"? I mean, I know there aren't many snow gnoblins in Rillia, but there are a few. They'll definitely have seen one before –'

'They might have seen a snow gnoblin before,' said a voice behind him, 'but never a fully armoured one.'

Mutt turned, and immediately slipped off the stool and on to the floor in pure shock at what he saw standing in the doorway behind him. Unfortunately, he'd sat right on one of Nissassa's daggers, which was hugely uncomfortable, but he was too startled to care, or even – for a long moment – to actually breathe.

There were many different clans of snow gnoblin, inhabiting vast areas of mountain, forest and frozen tundra in the lands far, far to the south of Rillia. They were fiercely independent, deeply intelligent and mainly peaceful unless attacked, in which case they would defend their lands with extraordinary ferocity. And, at those times, warriors of each clan would don suits of armour that had been passed down through the generations. Snow gnoblin war armour was the most impenetrable ever invented. It was forged of different metals, of different weights and thicknesses, to keep each warrior completely protected from all attacks. It was also considered to be sacred, never to be carried beyond their borders on pain of banishment. When he left with Clarity, Mirko had taken his because, as we discovered earlier in the story, he was leaving anyway. Remember when he went back to get his stuff? That's what he went back for.

Fully armoured, Mirko had to duck right down to get into the main room of the shop. And when he stood upright, the tip of his polished metal helmet brushed the ceiling. The helm was what had caused Mutt to slip off his stool in alarm. It was fashioned into the head of a roaring, terrifying beast. Lenses of crystal covered Mirko's eyes, and below them a fringe of sharp metal teeth covered the rest of his face. His arms, legs and chest were completely covered in metal plates, some bright polished silver, others copper or gold-coloured. He looked unstoppable. If you were a warrior and you saw that coming at you, you'd immediately start considering a career change. Which, of course, was the idea.

'Not bad,' said Nissassa, looking up at him critically. 'I reckon if you do a bit of roaring and stuff, they'll send every guard they've got to the castle gates.'

'Roaring,' said Mirko, 'is one of my specialities. My father taught me to roar,' he added. Mutt thought he detected tears brimming in the gnoblin's large yellow eyes behind the thick lenses, and for a moment he felt a stab to the heart, a flash of the deep sadness of a fellow being who has left their home behind forever. 'Right!' Mirko straightened his shoulders with a screech of metal plates rubbing together. 'Grab that jester. Let's get going before people start waking up. I might just attract a bit of attention walking through Meandermart like this.'

Mirko did indeed cut a memorable figure striding

through the city towards the castle. Mutt thought he would never forget the feeling of mingled pride, excitement and terror as they strode through the freezing, misty morning. Nissassa walked on his other side, elegant and silent as a cat, with the limp form of Handy Dandy draped over her shoulder as if the fairly plump jester was nothing more than a light jacket. Near the Knights' Academy they stopped in a side street.

'This is where I leave you,' said Mirko with a grim smile behind the rows of metal teeth. 'When you hear screaming, the distraction has begun.'

'See you inside, my old friend.' Nissassa spoke with unusual warmth.

It suddenly hit Mutt that what they were about to do was incredibly dangerous. 'You'll be all right, won't you?' he asked Mirko nervously.

A deep chuckle came from beneath the helmet. 'It's the guards you want to worry about, not me. Now, go! Get into position. And good luck!' The enormous armoured figure clanged off into the fog.

'Right, Mutt,' said Nissassa. 'You know the quickest way to the moat, I'm sure. Lead on!'

Mutt, with a brief flash of pride that this deadly

assassin girl (semi-retired) was relying on him for directions, looked about, getting his bearings. They weren't far away from the Oxbow Moat, the large semicircular lake that protected the northern part of Meandermart Castle, the cliffs rising from its calm waters right up to the ramparts above. 'This way,' he told Nissassa, and they set off quietly through the back streets.

Hardly anybody was about yet. There were a few brief glimpses of gnangers slinking out of sight round corners, some of them still chewing on the rubbish they'd been feasting on overnight. After ten minutes of weaving through the maze of houses and shops, they reached the edge of the wide park that fringed the moat.

'Softly now,' Nissassa warned, leading him out and round the edge of a lawn, the frozen grass crackling underfoot. At the very edge of the moat was a patch of tall oaks and hornbeams, planted to provide shade for picnicking Meandermartins in the warmer months. Now the trees were drooping and sad-looking, their bare branches frosted with white crystals. Beyond them was the Oxbow Moat itself, frozen solid until the spring thaw, still months away.

'What now?' said Mutt in a whisper, eyeing the other side of the frozen moat and the steep, rocky slope that soared upward to the distant shape of the castle, half hidden in mist and darkness.

'Now,' said Nissassa, 'we wait. And then we climb.' She dumped Handy Dandy on the ground and settled herself down with her back against a tree trunk. Rummaging in her bag, she pulled out a hunk of bread and tore off a large piece. 'Eat,' she told Mutt. 'Eat and rest. You'll need your strength soon.'

'What if he wakes up?' asked Mutt edgily, eyeing the sleeping jester.

'If he wakes up, then we're really in trouble.' She pointed up with a thumb, towards the castle. 'If he wakes up, it means the nyterra has taken on a new form. And that can't be good news for anybody. Now stop asking questions and eat your bread.' And Mutt, wrapping himself more tightly in his cloak, obediently did both those things.

Dawn broke reluctantly over the frozen city, the sun keeping its distance behind layers of mist and cloud. Gradually a vague greyish light filled the streets, and the citizens awoke to a full day of feasting and complaining. Moaningtide had come round once again. Winter was only half over, and everybody was enjoying being thoroughly miserable about it. 'Still months until spring,' they said as they greeted each other. 'I'm not sure I can stand it. It's cold all the time and it feels like it's only light for about three hours a day.'

Inside Meandermart Castle, preparations for the feast were now well underway, with cooks running back and forth whipping, baking, roasting and frosting for all they were worth. At the towers guarding the steep causeway outside, grumpy guards wished each other a miserable Moaningtide, marking the official start of the day.

'Commiserations of the season to you,' said one guard to another as they puffed and jiggled on the tower battlements, shuffling their feet in an effort to keep warm.

'A truly miserable one to you too,' replied the second guard automatically. 'And an Unhappy New Year . . . What's that?' He leaned out, squinting to see better through the flat early-morning light, which hadn't yet driven away the clinging night-time mist. A vague shape was moving up the wide street towards the towers. It loomed hugely through the fog, too big to be a person. The guard thought it must be a cart or a carriage of some kind, perhaps come to deliver last-minute supplies for the Moaningtide banquet.

'What *is* that?' repeated the first guard, also leaning out over the parapet. 'Whatever it is, it's coming this way,' he said with a slight sigh. 'Come on, we'd better go down and see who's up and about this early in the morning.'

By the time they had wound their way down the spiral staircase inside the tower and stepped out into the road, the shape had come much closer. And it was now obvious that, while it was still far too big to be a person, it was certainly no carriage or farm cart either.

'**Halt, stranger!**' bellowed the guard in his best and most intimidating who-goes-there voice. '**Identify yourself! State your business!**'

'I'm here to storm the castle,' came the reply out of the mist. 'I really suggest you get out of my way, because you seem nice and I don't want to hurt you.'

The guard attempted to give a scornful laugh, but it came out wrong and he quickly turned it into a cough. **'Don't be a fool!'** he shouted. 'Meandermart Castle is impregnable!'

'You're only saying that because it's never been pregnabated before,' replied the voice. 'Honestly, you really should get out of the way.'

'I am a proud soldier of the castle guard and I will never desert my post upon pain of – **GAAAARGH!** What in the name of Lepp the Liar is **THAT?!'**

(The Legend of Lepp the Liar is a popular fireside story in Rillia. It concerns a man called, as the title suggests, Lepp the Liar, who is actually quite truthful, but nobody ever believes him on account of his unfortunate name. He goes through a series of incredible adventures but then gets laughed at when he tries to tell people about them. It's both funny and tragic, but there isn't time to tell you any more about it here because things are about to get pretty exciting . . .)

The guard took a few staggering steps back and drew his sword as the huge shape loomed above him. Finally, when it was mere metres away, the fog thinned enough for him to make out a terrifying metal face above a gigantic armoured body. 'I warn you!' he squeaked, his voice refusing to work in anything but a high-pitched whistle (which startled a passing bat that had stayed up unusually late, but didn't even reach Mirko's ears). 'Stop or be *a-ttungh . . .*' said the guard weakly, trailing off as a large fist hit him squarely on the head. He fell sideways with a noise like saucepans being tipped into a bath.

Mirko turned to the other guard. 'Run up the hill and tell your friends I'm coming, would you?' he said conversationally.

The guard didn't hesitate. He turned smartly and took off for the Strangers' Tower as fast as his feet would carry him. It wasn't especially fast, given his armour – it's hard to run in armour unless, of course, you're a hugely strong snow gnoblin with a suit of armour that's been specially made from some of the rarest metals in existence. Not that Mirko wanted to run anywhere at this stage. He wanted to give the guard time to spread the word that the castle was under attack.

'THE CASTLE IS UNDER ATTACK!' squealed

the guard obligingly, as he pelted up the steep causeway towards the twin towers that guarded the final approach to the main gates. 'Call out the guards!'

'How many guards should I call out?' came an answering shout from the tower ramparts.

'All of them!' he screeched. **'All the guards! Every single guard that is available to come and do guarding! Call them all out! Quick! It's coming!'**

'What's coming?' The captain of the guard, a grizzled woman who had fought almost all the things that could be fought in her long years of service, looked keenly down the slope to try to make out the threat.

'I don't know what it is,' came the frightened peep from below. 'But it's big. It's really, really big. And even though it's kind of polite, it says it's going to storm the castle. And it knocked Zerin out cold! With its hand!'

The captain of the castle guard turned to her deputy. She spoke quietly, so as not to start a panic. 'Call out the guards,' she told him.

'Which guards?'

'All of them.'

'All of them?'

'Yes, you heard what that guard said. We need all of them. Now. Quickly.' The deputy scuttled off down the stairs and ran off towards the main gates, screaming at the top of his voice and rather spoiling the captain's plan to avoid panic:

'WE'RE UNDER ATTACK! ALL GUARDS TO THE MAIN GATE! PANIC STATIONS! EVERYBODY, PANIC!'

Word quickly spread throughout Meandermart Castle, and from everywhere guards hurried towards the main gate, deserting their usual posts. Which, of course, was the plan. Because many of those posts were the archers' positions that overlooked the steep cliffs above the Oxbow Moat.

At the base of these cliffs, Nissassa sat calmly beside the frozen moat, her eyes closed and her mouth slightly open, which (pro tip) is an old assassin's trick to sharpen your hearing. Every so often she held up a hand for silence when Mutt shifted impatiently or drew in a breath in preparation for asking whether she could hear anything yet. Beside them, motionless on the ground except for his shallow breathing, lay the yellow-and-red-clad figure of Handy Dandy.

'It's started,' muttered Nissassa shortly.

They had been sitting there for two hours and Mutt was now cold in places where he hadn't even previously realized he had nerves. He thrust his head forward and concentrated with all his might, hoping that by straining hard enough he might be able to hear what was going on.

'What on earth are you doing?' she asked him.

'Trying to hear.'

Nissassa shook her head with a slight smile. 'Stop straining like that. You look like you're going to burst something. We train for years to sharpen our hearing.'

'Will you teach me?' Mutt had already been rather in awe of Nissassa, but today it seemed he was learning new cool skills from her every few minutes.

'If we get through this and rescue Clarity, thanks to your brainwave,' she told him, 'then you can ask me any favour. So, yes, if that's what you want – I'll teach you. Or start to, anyway. Like I said, it takes years.' She rose to her feet and pulled a small device from a pouch on her belt. Lifting it to her eye, she squinted up towards the castle.

'What's that?' Mutt got to his feet too. 'Is it magic?'

'Depends on your definition of magic,' she said with a shrug. 'It's an arrangement of small circles of glass, bent in an ingenious way to allow you to see things a great distance away.'

'Definitely magic,' Mutt decided.

'As you wish.' Nissassa snapped the telescope shut. (Not that she called it a telescope, but that's basically what it was.) And she bent to lift Handy Dandy up on to her shoulders, as easily as if he'd been a novelty inflatable jester. Not that they had those in Rillia either. 'Ready?' she asked Mutt.

'Ready to climb the terrifying cliffs to the heavily guarded castle, even though absolutely everybody agrees that it's impossible?' he asked. 'Aye, aye, sir.'

'Good.' She gave an approving nod. 'You don't lack bravery, at least.' She pulled a length of the soft black rope from her belt and firmly lashed the jester into position. 'You can hang on to this, Mutt, OK? Don't let go, whatever you do. Come on, quick – the archer towers are empty. Now's our chance.' And, moving with a stealth and grace completely unsuited to somebody with a jester tied across their shoulders, she stalked out across the frozen moat and stopped at the bottom of the grey cliffs, Mutt jogging to keep pace with her.

'Wrap your hands securely in the rope,' she told him, and Mutt took a firm grip on the two loops she had left conveniently hanging down her back, winding them round his wrists and giving a large and very nervous gulp into the bargain. 'Ready?' asked Nissassa again, pulling two black gloves from her belt and putting them on.

'Ready,' confirmed Mutt, peering curiously at the gloves. They had long metal claws that fastened securely round Nissassa's wrists and extended along each of her fingers. With them on, the black-clad assassin looked not unlike a nimble cat. And, exactly like a cat, she took a small leap upward on to the cliffs and began to climb. Mutt gasped and held on more tightly as he swung from side to side, but he soon found that, by planting his boots on the back of Nissassa's thick leather belt, he was able to keep his

CLARITY JONES AND THE MAGICAL DETECTIVE AGENCY

balance fairly well. The jester jiggled and flopped in front of his face as they inched higher and higher towards the castle.

At no point had Nissassa said to Mutt the words 'don't look down'. It's a pointless thing to say in situations like this, because what the other person always immediately does is, yep, look down. It's like saying, 'Don't think about a zebra dressed in a top hat doing a little tap dance.' See, you're already thinking about it, aren't you? Anyway, despite not having been explicitly told not to look down, Mutt was well aware that in situations like this, perched on a perilously high cliff, it's not advisable to look down. But he was also aware that he was never likely to be in this situation again, and he was a boy who liked to make the most of any experience that came his way. So, half closing his eyes against the cold air that seemed to rise up from the frozen moat, he looked down.

Bad idea. Mutt's head swam as the panorama of the city spread out below him, picked out in the grey and white tones of a freezing midwinter dawn. The moat lay directly below, looking like something you really wouldn't want to fall on to. Next to it, the trees and lawns of the park were white and ghostly beneath crystals of ice. And, beyond that, the streets, towers and rooftops of the city of Meandermart stretched away to the high city walls. By now, everybody was up and about, wishing each other a miserable Moaningtide. They bustled through the streets like insects. Smoke rose from the chimneys and Mutt's breakfast also rose. He swallowed and fixed his eyes on what was above instead, watching Nissassa's arms as she pulled them tirelessly upward. If there's one thing you develop working as an assassin, it's really seriously impressive upper-body strength.

As they climbed higher still, Mutt's ears began to pick out a strange collection of sounds. There were shouts, thudding footsteps, the clang of metal on metal, and an odd tinkling, like hailstones falling on a metal roof. It was, in fact, the sound of numerous arrows hitting Mirko's armour and pinging off in different directions. Already, more than a few guards had been hit by ricochets. Mirko was still walking slowly and unstoppably towards the castle gates, flinging the castle's defenders behind him and parrying their sword blows with his metal-clad arms. No matter how many times he was told the story afterwards – and that was a lot, because he demanded it be told on a daily basis for at least two months straight – Mutt never ceased to be sad that he wasn't there to see the March of the Marauding Meandermart Monster on Moaningtide Morn. There are actually now several popular songs about it – the minstrels had a field day. (They love a good monster attack, minstrels.)

THE GREAT ESCAPE

In the dungeons, Clarity Jones sat in her customary position, legs dangling over the cliff edge at the back of room twelve, and listened. Bayler the jailer had already made his morning rounds flinging pieces of stew on bread into each cell. He'd been in an even more polite mood than usual today, asking if her bed was quite comfortable and whether she was enjoying her stay. He'd completely ignored her replies, of course, which had been less than complimentary. But, once he'd gone, Clarity had settled down to do what she'd been doing the past few days: waiting and thinking. She was excellent at both those things.

Even without the benefit of visiting Gabriel

Ratchets the monster catcher, Clarity Jones had worked out that the person they had rescued from the merchant's house could not possibly be the real Handy Dandy. She had also worked out that this was a story in which two people hadn't behaved as expected: the jester and the underduke. She knew something very dark and dangerous was going on. And, when she had seen a large black bird flap past her cell, the picture of the nyterra in Mirko's book had come back to her. *I wonder* . . . she thought.

So now she sat on the cliff edge, peering down at the city far below, thinking about her friends. She thought about Mirko mopping the floor, and Nissassa sharpening her daggers. And she thought about Mutt, the lonely boy she'd taken in. A boy who was keen to help, and keen to learn. A boy who, like her, had lost his family and needed a new one. And Clarity

Jones smiled to herself as she wondered which of them would be the one to crack the case first. Because she knew, with calm confidence, that one of them would. And so, when she heard shouts and running feet from the battlements far above her, a slow smile broke out across her face. It sounded like something was happening. The game was afoot.

Getting to her feet, Clarity Jones once again delved into the hidden pocket inside her belt and pulled out the folded piece of jet-black cloth. Shaking it out, she revealed a largish circle of material, which shimmered oddly in the light spilling into the cell. Carefully, she placed the black circle on the floor just to one side of the door and listened to the growing sounds of panic from above her. Her grin grew wider still.

At what he liked to fondly think of as the dungeon reception desk, Bayler the jailer sat writing carefully in his large leather-bound notebook.

Afternoon service completed, he wrote in his neat, slanting handwriting. *Today the guests enjoyed another portion of my famous stew on bread, although Horace in cell eight appeared to be slightly disappointed. Instead of eating his delicious repast, he smeared the stew all over his body and threw the bread back out of his cell along with several extremely rude words.*

He paused in his writing as a shout echoed down the passageway from the cell block: 'Help!'

Bayler frowned. He was quite used to his prisoners shouting all kinds of things, mainly variations on 'Let me out!' or 'I'm innocent!' or 'I'm going mad!' or 'Don't you have anything besides stew on bread?'. Over his many years as jailer (or 'cell services facilitator', as he preferred to define it to himself), he'd got used to ignoring all these cries. But the voice that was calling out now was an unexpected one. It was the voice of his newest guest, the lady in cell twelve.

'Did someone shout **"Help!"**?' enquired Bayler, leaning out through his hatch to shout down the passageway.

'Yes,' confirmed the same voice. '**Help!**' it added again.

Reluctantly, Bayler collected the right key from the rack behind him and lumbered down the passageway to the door of cell twelve. Bending forward, he grasped the bars set into the stout wooden door and peered through. After a moment, he reached up and rubbed his eyes with his fists before bending and peering through again. It just wasn't possible: the cell was completely empty!

'**Help!**' came the voice again. Perhaps it was just a trick of the echoes off the stone, but it sounded like it came from the far side of the room – over the edge of the steep cliff that led to nowhere except the rocky shores of the Oxbow Moat far below.

'Did you fall off the cliff?' asked Bayler.

'I fell off the cliff,' confirmed the voice of Clarity Jones, adding yet another '**Help!**' for good measure.

Bayler sighed. This did happen occasionally. Mainly, though, it was when prisoners went mad and simply flung themselves off the cliff. In those cases, they always met a sticky end so didn't need rescuing. But, every now and then, one of his guests would slip and fall over the edge, and manage somehow to cling on for dear life to the rocky surface. Sighing still more deeply, the jailer unlocked the cell door and strode over to the other side, where he leaned carefully forward, peering over the edge.

'Where are you?' he asked suspiciously. 'I can't see you.'

'That's because you're not looking in an unexpected place,' replied a voice from behind him.

Bayler jumped and had to flail his huge arms to regain his balance, windmilling them frantically as he teetered dangerously on the cliff edge. Once he'd found his feet, he wheeled round on the spot to see Clarity Jones standing calmly in the doorway. She had emerged from a large hole in the rock floor, just to one side of the door. And, as he watched, she picked up the hole, folded it carefully and placed it back in one of her pockets.

'Portable hole,' she explained to him as she did so. 'Very useful hiding place. You really should get one.'

'That's . . .' Bayler gaped. 'That's impossible!'

'The impossible is my speciality,' replied Clarity Jones with a smile. 'Enjoy your stay,' she added, and quickly slammed the door closed and locked it firmly behind her. 'There's a lovely bed, running water and spectacular views. Just shout if you need anything, won't you?' And with that, her face disappeared from the barred window.

'Hey, let me out!' bellowed Bayler, rushing to the door and tugging desperately at the bars. **'I'm innocent!'**

'*I'm* innocent!' came a shout from further down the corridor. 'Let *me* out!'

'Let me out too!' added another one of the prisoners. And soon they were all shouting more or less the same thing, except Horace in cell eight, who was shouting, 'I'm a cheeky little orange called Susan!' But, as we know, he'd gone completely mad some time ago.

Higher up Meandermart Castle, in her luxurious apartments above the throne room, the Duchess Peruka was blissfully unaware that anything strange was going on. She was busy preparing herself for the great banquet that would start at breakfast time and go on for the entire day. Her faithful fool Handy Dandy was at hand, as always. He sat to one side as her servants primped and painted her long face. But instead of being entertaining, which was literally his job, he was slumped silently forward with a morose expression. 'You haven't even wished me a mournful Moaningtide, Dandy dear,' said the duchess with a purse of her purple lips.

'What?' The jester had been staring at her intently in the mirror. 'Oh, sorry.' He sat up straight and thought for a moment. 'Er, fol de-diddle. Faith. Egad,' he said unenthusiastically. 'Complaints of the season to you, Your Marvellousness.'

The duchess frowned irritably. Ever since he'd been rescued, Handy Dandy had been noticeably less funny. He'd also developed the very unnerving habit of watching her constantly from all angles. (The previous day she'd even caught him standing in front of a large and very detailed painting of her that hung in the throne room, looking at it intently while making a strange growling noise. When she'd questioned him sharply, he had leaped into the air with an expression of fury, before realizing who she was, giving a rather forced laugh and falling over. 'Just admiring your likeness, my lady . . . foregad,' he had burbled from the floor.) Her frown deepened. Something had definitely gone wrong with him during his captivity. She let out a sigh. Alongside everything else, it was now looking like she'd have to train up a new jester. *A duchess's work is never done*, she thought miserably to herself as two servants entered, tottering beneath the weight of the huge and elaborate Moaningtide wig she'd commissioned to surprise the king. It was shaped like a traditional

Moaningtide tree, made from green wool and dotted with tiny candles in brass holders. It was imposing. It was expensive. It was the most ridiculously dangerous fire risk you ever saw.

Elsewhere in the chilly, winding hallways of Meandermart Castle, the duchess's brother was not nearly so calm. Underduke Ferdinand had awoken early and started pacing through his richly decorated chambers, anxiety gnawing at his stomach. You'll know all about this too if you're a secret villain – the day you put your villainous plan into operation is always fairly nerve-racking. There's so much that can – and usually does – go wrong with villainous plans, you see. Heroes turning up at the last moment, giving you your comeuppance in a dramatic fashion, that kind of thing. So it's perhaps understandable that the underduke was nervously pacing – pacing so pacily that his tracks could clearly be seen in the thick, deep-red carpet by the time dawn broke on Moaningtide morn.

Underduke Ferdinand's restless roaming wasn't made any more comfortable when the guards suddenly started running around the castle uttering frenzied cries of 'We're under attack!', 'To the gates!

To the gates!' and, at one point, 'Ayieeeeee!' (which is never a good sign). He stalked to the door and jerked it open. 'You, there!' he barked at an archer who was dashing past looking pale and nervous. 'What's going on?'

'All guards called to the main gates, Your Under-Marvellousness,' responded the guard as he dashed past. 'There's some kind of monster on the causeway!'

The underduke rolled his eyes. Typical. Who could this monster be? Not a hero, he hoped. He thought he'd seen off those annoying troublemakers who'd unwittingly helped him with his plan. He'd managed to reassure himself that the meddling detective who'd asked too many awkward questions was safely in the dungeons. 'Oh bother,' he muttered to himself crossly. 'Whatever's at the gate,' he shouted out loud at the archer's retreating back, 'slay it! Stick it so full of arrows that it resembles a hedge-hawk!'

CREATURES OF THE TRULY TERRIFYING FOREST

HEDGE~HAWKS

*H*edge~hawks are large birds of prey that have developed a forest of sharp spines on their back. They attack prey by stopping in mid~flight and dropping on small animals, spines downwards. Occasionally, they fall on people's heads, which can be extremely uncomfortable and has led to the development of the distinctive Rillian hat, which is made of unusually thick cloth.

Underduke Ferdinand closed his door again and pondered. Clearly, something was going wrong. 'Calm yourself, Ferdinand,' he said in a soothing tone. 'You've planned for every eventuality. This castle is impregnable. Nobody can stop you.' Unfortunately for him, all three of these statements were wholly inaccurate. 'But perhaps, just to be sure . . .' he muttered, wringing his hands together. 'I should accelerate the plan slightly. Yes, yes, that's it.' Having made his decision, he marched to the door and disappeared down the passageway.

Duchess Peruka was distracted from her thoughts of jester-firing by a knock at her chamber door. 'See who that is,' she told Handy Dandy curtly, and he picked himself up from the floor with a mutinous expression and went to see who it was.

'Are you ready?' asked Underduke Ferdinand in a whisper, relieved to see that the nyterra was already in position. The creature that looked exactly like Handy Dandy nodded with a satisfied smile. 'Excellent,' said the underduke. 'In that case, I have decided to put our plan into action now, immediately, instead of during the feast. Prepare yourself!' In a louder voice he said, 'It is only I, dear sister! Come to wish you a mournful Moaningtide and many miserable days of winter still to come.' He swept dramatically into the room. 'Could you give my sister and me a few moments alone, please?' he asked the assembled servants with an imperious wave of his hand, and they began to bustle out of the room.

'What are you doing?' demanded Duchess Peruka. 'Don't send them all away! I'm not ready for the banquet! I need at least another two layers of powder on my face, and what about the wig?' The two wig-carriers had carefully set the giant green pyramid down in a corner and were scurrying for the door.

'Patience, sister, patience,' said Ferdinand airily. 'There's plenty of time. And I have a seasonal surprise for you. A very, very special surprise. It's going to absolutely stun you, I guarantee it.'

'Very well, very well,' agreed the duchess, mollified. She loved surprises. 'Wait outside, all of you,' she called after the departing servants. 'I'll need to continue my preparations as soon as my brother has surprised me.' She waited patiently while everyone left. Duchesses have a great many servants, so it took a few minutes. But eventually the chamber door closed, leaving Duchess Peruka alone with only the underduke and Handy Dandy. Which, considering one of them was plotting to have her killed and the other was a terrifying shapeshifting monster, was a peculiarly bad idea even by her standards.

As we now know, the nyterra needed to spend a great deal of time observing someone or something before it could transform. In the days since it had entered the castle, this particular beast, in the form of Handy Dandy, had been staring more or less constantly at Duchess Peruka. And now it was ready. 'Close your eyes, sister dear,' said Ferdinand, 'and get ready for the surprise of your life.' With a smug little smile of anticipation, she obeyed, turning back to her dressing table and putting her hands over her face.

Behind her, her brother nodded to the nyterra, which began to transform. With a sickly creaking, cracking sound, Handy Dandy expanded, breaking open like an engorged overripe fruit. The yellow and red of the jester's costume was absorbed by stretches of black, burned-looking skin. And, after a few moments, where the jester had stood there now crouched the nyterra in its true form. It looked not unlike a monstrous bat, with leathery, tattered wings

folded tight against its body. For a moment, it held
that shape, its long, beaked face gazing at the duchess's
back with a look of malevolent concentration. Then,
with a shimmering of iridescent colours across its
skin, it slowly morphed into an exact replica of
Peruka. If you'd been there, it would have freaked
you out quite considerably. But, luckily, you weren't
there – if you had been, the evil underduke would
probably have thrown you out of the window.

'Open your eyes,' trilled Ferdinand in a sing-song
voice. And, with a coy little giggle, Duchess Peruka
(the real one) lifted her hands from her face and

peered into the mirror to see what the strange noises behind her had been all about. Who knows what she had been expecting (it's hard to buy presents for duchesses as they tend to already have absolutely everything they desire). But she certainly hadn't been expecting to look in the mirror and see *herself* standing in the middle of the room behind her, smiling a wicked smile. For a split second, her brain tried to process what was going on. Some kind of trick mirror? But remember, Reader: once the nyterra had taken on your form, you were destined to fall into a deep swoon from which you would not awake until it changed into a new shape. And so, just as the beginnings of a really impressively big scream were starting to form on her face, Duchess Peruka slumped forward on to her dressing table, out cold.

'Quickly,' said Ferdinand to the other duchess. 'Put her in the wardrobe and call the servants back in. Finish getting ready for the banquet while I go and see what's happening at the gate. And, remember –' he added, pausing at the door – 'on my signal, attack the king. Got it?'

'Got it,' replied the fake duchess, dragging her doppelgänger into the wardrobe and shutting the door firmly. 'And then you'll release me?'

'I give you my word,' promised Ferdinand, turning the door handle. 'You may continue,' he told the cluster of staff outside. 'But I warn you, she's in a terrible temper.'

'Get in here and primp me!' came a petulant shriek from inside. 'Come on, come on, you idiots!'

Now we have to return to the outside of the castle.

Not the gates, where Mirko's armour is still being hit by hundreds of arrows, not one of which stands any chance of doing him any damage. We need to return to the steep cliffs below the northern castle walls, where, if you remember, Nissassa is slowly climbing, with Mutt strapped to her back below the unconscious Handy Dandy (real version). At least, he had been unconscious. Remember that sentence a few paragraphs back? The one about 'a deep swoon from which you would not awake until it changed into a new shape'? Yeah. So, about that . . .

'Almost – *puff* – there,' grunted Nissassa over her shoulder, lifting one of her metal-clawed gloves and searching for a crack in the grey rock. With a tiny scraping sound, she found purchase and, tensing her shoulders, pulled them up another few inches. Mutt, who was still determinedly not looking down, could see that, not far above them, the rock began to give way to blocks of lighter stone. These were the lower walls of Meandermart Castle, built right into the cliff face hundreds of years before.

They were, indeed, almost there. Almost about to achieve the impossible. They were about to become the first people ever to sneak into Meandermart

Castle the back way.

'WE-AAAAARRRRRGGGGGHHHHHH!' said Handy Dandy suddenly, opening his eyes and finding himself strapped to an assassin's back near the top of a gigantic scary cliff. 'WA-RAAAARRRRRGH! Hah! Hah! FLE-EEARRRGGGHHHH!'

'Shh! Please stop making sounds!' pleaded Mutt as the jester wriggled and gibbered.

'And please stop moving about,' added Nissassa through gritted teeth, holding on as best she could. 'If he makes us fall,' she added, glancing down at the frozen moat far below, 'that will be the least funny thing he's ever done. And by all accounts that's up against some pretty stiff competition.'

'WHO ARE YOU?' squeaked the jester, seeing Mutt hanging on to the loops of rope below him.

'My name's Mutt,' replied Mutt in the most jester-soothing tone of voice he could manage. 'My friends and I are detectives, and –'

'What's a detective?' replied Handy Dandy automatically, before his mind was overtaken by more urgent questions. 'Why are we on a cliff?' he said in a shrill, desperate voice. 'Why am I tied up? Where have I been? I was in bed and the . . . the cat . . . it changed! It changed into a monster!' His words were coming out faster and faster, his eyes wide and his mouth gaping.

'Nissassa,' said Mutt grimly, 'I think we have a jester panic situation developing here.' But another skill that you develop as a really top assassin is the ability to remain calm under pressure. With a superhuman effort, Nissassa withdrew one of her gloves from a crevice in the rock and flung herself upward, finding purchase higher up the cliff. With Handy Dandy still gibbering about cat monsters, gigantic claws and flying out of the window, she climbed even faster up towards the lowest windows of the castle. Ignoring the jerking and fidgeting of the full-scale jester freak-out happening on her shoulders, she kept going until, with a final bicep-burning lunge, she pulled up and over a wide stone parapet, letting all three of them slump on to the cold floor of a rarely used storeroom on the very lowest level of Meandermart Castle.

'Gaining access to the castle from cliffside,' said Nissassa as she fumbled with the knots binding Handy Dandy to her back, 'is now, officially, no longer impossible.'

CHAPTER 12

WORST. BANQUET. EVER.

Complain, complain all over the town,
The sky it is grey and the mud it is brown.
It gets really dark by a quarter past three,
Oh won't you all come and moan with me?

As the minstrels struck up the traditional gripe that opened the Moaningtide commiserations, the doors of the great banqueting hall were flung wide. A long table stretched the entire length of the room, lit with candles and groaning under the weight of countless silver platters bearing rich foodstuffs from all across the known world. There were roasted haunches of moxen, fried hedge-hawk bellies in spicy sauce, and even dishes of a rare delicacy – delicious Bethcar pears from a strange, inaccessible land to the north-east. When an actual king is visiting, you're expected to pull out all the stops.

To the mournful sound of trumpets, King Bernard of Rillia appeared in the doorway and surveyed the piled platters with a peculiar feeling in his tummy. When he was a younger man he really used to enjoy a good banquet. But since he'd lost his queen he found eating more of a chore than anything else. But – he sighed a little to himself – the Duchess of Meandermart had clearly gone to a lot of effort to impress him. He'd have to make a good show of enjoying himself. At least, as it was Moaningtide, he wouldn't be expected to smile. That was something.

There was another minor-key *toot* from the trumpeters, another set of doors opened at the far end of the hall, and Duchess Peruka stepped into view. She was wearing the enormous tree-shaped wig, all its candles now lit. No fewer than three servants with poles were stationed around her, bracing themselves frantically to keep it upright. 'The worst day of the entire year has arrived!' said

301

the duchess in a ringing tone that made the glasses vibrate. 'I invite you to come and share with me your complaints about this, the darkest and coldest part of the winter.'

'That sounds absolutely miserable.' The king gave the traditional reply in his most formal, kingly voice, wondering how long he'd have to make polite conversation before he could escape and sit in his room looking gloomily out of the window, which is what he spent most of his private hours doing these days. He was so caught up in this thought that he didn't even notice that the duchess was regarding him with an expression that hovered somewhere between pure hatred and complete disgust.

'Then come sit and moan with me,' replied the thing that looked exactly like Duchess Peruka, completing the exchange of Moaningtide formalities. With a traditional grimace, King Bernard plodded into the hall and took the seat of honour. There was a third, final and even sadder-sounding *blart!* from the trumpeters, and the rest of the guests began filing in: rich merchants, visiting dignitaries and some minor nobles from the outlying towns to the west. At their head came Underduke Ferdinand, nodding politely to the people on either side of him as he moved towards the head of the table, and laughing a silent, invisible and very evil laugh deep in the centre of his wicked heart. Within an hour, his sister would be facing execution and he would be Warden of Meandermart. *And why stop there?* he thought greedily to himself. Who knew where the gratitude of a king might take him?

All around the sides of the hall, candles blazed on the branches of Moaningtide trees beside small slips of parchment with complaints about winter written on them. *My pig died of cold*, read one of them. *An icicle fell on my grandad*, moaned another. The minstrels broke into another mournful gripe:

It will be cold for twenty more weeks.
With a moaning, a moaning, a moaning-o.
The winter is so long and bleak.
With a moaning, a moaning, a rubbishy-o.

The feast began. As is traditional on Moaningtide Day, the guests only spoke about the things they hated most about winter. Many had stories to share about terrible things that had happened to them at this most hated time of the year. One merchant had hobbled in on wooden crutches and spent fully half an hour regaling his neighbours with the tale of how he'd slipped over on an icy puddle. They shook their heads sympathetically. 'Commiserations of the season to you,' they murmured politely, stuffing their faces all the while.

Underduke Ferdinand was enjoying the feast enormously. It's amazing how making evil plans and carrying them out can sharpen your appetite. He merrily stuffed himself with all manner of treats, growing redder in the face and more excited as he contemplated the chaos that was about to erupt. He glanced around the room as the guests swapped tales of wintertime woe and gradually ate themselves into a stupor.

Nearby, King Bernard was nibbling half-heartedly at a slice of berry pie. 'Not hungry, Your Majesty?' shouted one purple-nosed merchant, waving his goblet and slopping rich red wine over his sleeve. The king gave a weak smile in reply and took another bite of pie, not noticing the duchess, or rather the nyterra, who was now glaring at him with a quite open expression of hatred.

The underduke saw it, though, and smiled to himself. *Soon*, he thought. *Any moment now.*

At the front of the castle, the remaining guards had formed into a tight defensive phalanx against the stout, high wooden gates. Mirko was still advancing ponderously towards them, the weak sunlight glinting off his terrifying armour.

'Stand your ground!' the captain of the castle guard urged the others. 'Stand your ground! The castle must be protected at all costs.'

Another fusillade of arrows shrieked through the cold air, *ting*ing harmlessly off the metal plates and falling to the ground, which was now thick with spent arrows.

Just before it reached the castle's last defenders, the gigantic armoured figure stopped, its head tilted as it squinted up at the sky, judging the time by the pale sun that was now dimly visible through the thin layers of high white cloud. 'Well, I reckon that should have given them enough time,' said Mirko to himself in a satisfied tone of voice. 'Yep, I think that should just about do it. Right . . .' And, turning on his heel, he began to stomp back down the causeway, pausing every now and then to say 'sorry' to some of the more badly injured guards who were lying on one side or other of the path, many of them groaning with pain.

The guard captain was astounded. 'Oi!' she shouted after him. 'Aren't you going to attack the castle any more?'

'No, you're all right,' came the reply from the huge, lumbering figure as it retreated. 'I've changed my mind. Mournful Moaningtide to you.'

'Commiserations of the season,' she shouted back automatically, before collecting herself. 'Well . . . and don't come back!' she yelled defiantly, deciding that she may as well chalk this one up as a victory for the castle guard.

'Well done! Well done!' she cried to the castle guards (the remaining standing-up ones at least, the ones whose limbs all still worked). 'We've fought off the beast! This is a glorious triumph!'

'He said he'd changed his mind,' one of the guards contradicted her.

'**Shut up,**' she snapped.

Mirko's distraction had, indeed, given his friends enough time to get inside the castle. Their only challenge now was to remain undetected – and that's not easy when you've got a panicking jester to contend with. Handy Dandy had spent a great deal of time saying things like 'a-feff, a-feff, a feff' and hyperventilating, as Mutt tried to explain what had been going on for the past few days while he'd been asleep in the merchant's cellar.

'The underduke?' said the jester eventually. They had finally persuaded him to stop pacing round the storeroom and sit down on a stool. 'Underduke Ferdinand? Plotting against his sister?'

'Yes,' Mutt confirmed for the eighth time. 'We think he means to attack the king.'

'The king?' Handy Dandy's mouth hung open slackly. 'King Bernard?'

'How many kings are there in Rillia?' demanded Nissassa, losing her patience. 'Yes, King Bernard. *The* king.'

'But, but, but . . .' The jester ran out of words briefly. 'Tell me again about this monster,' he said when he'd found some words again.

At this, Nissassa stalked over and grabbed him by the shoulders. '**There. Is. NO. TIME. To. Explain. It. All. To. You. Again,**' she told him, punctuating each word with a firm shake that made the bells on his hat jingle madly. 'You need to trust us –' *Jingle jangle*. 'You need to stop panicking –' *Jingle*. 'You need to show us where the dungeons are. Right –' *jingle* – 'now.' *Jingle jangle jingle*.

Back upstairs at the banquet, Underduke Ferdinand noticed one of the castle guards sneak in by a side door, looking red-faced and nervous, and take up her usual position at the side of the hall. Impatiently, he beckoned her over. 'What's been going on out there?' he hissed when she had bustled over.

'There was, ahem, a small attack on the gates, Your Under-Marvellousness,' the guard told him in a whisper. 'It's all been contained. No need to worry your sister or the king.'

'Who attacked the gates?' The underduke didn't like the sound of this one bit.

'It was –' the guard looked nervously up and down the table, and bent her head to avoid being overheard – 'some kind of large monster, with armour on.'

Underduke Ferdinand thought fast. He'd seen a large creature recently. That hulking brute that had been with the detective. Why hadn't he imprisoned the lot of them when he'd had the chance? He cursed under his breath as he got the first inkling that he might have been guilty of a classic bad-guy error: underestimating his enemy. 'But you defeated the creature?' he hissed. The guard nodded with a proud smile. 'It has been slain?' he asked.

'Er . . .' As the guard hesitated, Ferdinand got up from the table abruptly. Grabbing the guard by the arm, he hustled her over to the wall, where there was no chance they could be overheard.

'What do you mean, "er"?' he snarled angrily. 'Somebody attacks the castle gates; you slay them! You literally have one job as a castle guard, and that's it! Guard gates. Slay intruders.'

'Technically that's two jobs,' began the guard, but his furious expression stopped her in her tracks. 'The, er, the beast ceased its attack after we pelted it with arrows,' she said, attempting to put a gloss on what had happened to make the Castle Guard seem less useless. 'It . . . it surrendered. Well, it fled, at a walking pace, back down the hill,' she admitted. 'Which is the same thing as surrendering, if you really think about it.'

'Get some other guards,' he told her, gripping her arm so tightly that her chain mail left a pattern on her skin that was there until the following Wednesday. 'And cover all the doors to this banqueting chamber. Nobody comes in. **NOBODY. Get it?'**

'What about the servants?' she asked. 'What if somebody needs to go out and use the garderobe?'

(Quick note: the garderobe is a castle toilet. It's basically a stone seat with a hole in it, positioned over the edge of the cliffs. Luckily not the part that Nissassa had just climbed up.)

'What don't you understand,' said the underduke in a deceptively calm voice, 'about the word "nobody"?'

'So . . . nobody?' clarified the guard. 'Not anybody? What about the minstrels?'

'Bah!' Ferdinand's patience, which was already at breaking point, snapped like a dry twig that had just been stepped on by an elephant made of pure annoyance. '**NO. BOH. DEE. No exceptions. No**

minstrels. No garderobe visits. No servants. Guard the doors and stop anybody from coming in. Go, go, go! Now, now, now! Or I will have you executed.'

This final argument was an excellent one and proved to be extremely persuasive. The guard clicked her heels together smartly and rushed for the door, and the underduke, shaking his head at the sheer amount of admin involved in plotting to have your sister killed, returned to the banqueting table and grabbed another wince pie to soothe his troubled nerves.

Before long, there were guards stationed at each door to the banqueting chamber. They looked battle-stained and weary after their struggle with Mirko out on the causeway, but they were heavily armoured and stood with drawn swords barring anybody from entering or leaving the room. King Bernard, who was listening intently to a very long and very miserable anecdote that a merchant was telling him about a distant cousin freezing to death while out hunting, completely failed to notice that anything was wrong. A few of the guests looked around nervously but felt it might be rude to enquire what was going on. And, besides, tradition dictated that the only topic of conversation at the great Moaningtide banquet had to be how miserable one was that the winter was only halfway done.

The minstrels up in their gallery struck up another gripe – the ever-depressing 'I Should Have Worn More Layers, Nay Nay the Nonny Nay'. The underduke gave a sly glance around the great hall to make sure all the doors were secure, and decided that the time was right to put his evil plan into action. The banquet had now been going on for some two hours, and several of the guests were starting to look rather full. He wanted to stage the attack on the king before they began to drop off. It wasn't uncommon for guests at the great banquet to place their heads on the table and sleep off their first few courses before waking to carry on eating and complaining. He looked across at Duchess Peruka – or rather the nyterra – caught its eye and gave a significant nod. The nyterra returned it, its eyes glinting coldly. The underduke felt a thrill of excitement. All these months of planning. All the hitches he'd encountered along the way. And now he was about to enjoy his moment of triumph. Everybody in this hall would witness him saving King Bernard's life. Just as long as nobody burst into the hall and shouted some dumb heroic thing, like 'Stop the banquet!'.

As you may have guessed, Underduke Ferdinand's day was about to go downhill extremely fast.

Let's get back to Mutt and Nissassa, who we last saw in the storeroom. Now that they'd managed to very slightly calm the real Handy Dandy down, the frightened-looking jester was leading them towards the dungeons. The bells on his hat jingled as they ran down seemingly endless stone staircases, but luckily the castle was still free of guards as they were either guarding the banqueting hall or out at the front gate and still barely conscious. Despite that, Nissassa remained on high alert as they scurried down, and when they heard footsteps pounding up the lowest staircase towards them, the assassin girl immediately sprang her sleeve daggers and crouched in a defensive position, Mutt and Handy Dandy cowering behind her. But instead of a phalanx of heavily armed guards, it was Clarity Jones who came running up the stairs towards them.

'Ah, you're here,' said Clarity matter-of-factly.

'Excellent. Well done. Right, shall we get on with solving the case?'

'You've escaped from the dungeons already!' said Nissassa, rising to her feet and stowing the daggers with an unconcealed air of disappointment. 'I thought that was supposed to be impossible.'

'The impossible is her speciality,' Mutt reminded Nissassa, grinning at Clarity.

'It is indeed,' the detective agreed. 'So – you found the real jester then, I see.' Handy Dandy, still pale-faced and shell-shocked, gave her a limp wave. 'Hmm.' Clarity Jones looked at him doubtfully. 'Not very funny, is he?'

'It certainly wasn't very funny when he woke up halfway up the cliff,' agreed Nissassa.

'You climbed the cliffs beneath Meandermart Castle?' Clarity raised her eyebrows respectfully.

'Looks like we're all specializing in the impossible today,' Nissassa told her proudly. 'But, to be fair, it was Mutt who reminded us about it. He ran into the shop, shouting, "Never eliminate the impossible!"'

'Did you?' Clarity Jones looked at him with approval. 'Excellent work. So you've worked out that there's a plot against the duchess? Is it the nyterra?'

Her eyes gleamed with excitement as the puzzle began to unravel.

'Yes, it's the nyterra,' Mutt confirmed. 'We got the monster catcher to admit he hadn't really killed it. I used your lie detonator – hope that's OK?'

'Just a drop, though, right?' Clarity looked slightly worried. 'It's some of my rarest magic, that. I think it's the last remaining supply in the whole world. But I'm sure there's lots left. Isn't there?'

Mutt, remembering how the entire bottle of liquid had spilled out, covered his embarrassment with a cough. Heartily glad he himself wasn't under the influence of lie detonator, he mumbled, 'Yeah, I'm sure there must be plenty left,' deciding this was a discussion that could wait for later.

'Right then,' said Clarity. 'Nissassa, did you bring enough daggers?'

'You can never have enough daggers,' the assassin girl reminded her. 'But I've got quite a few, yes.'

'In that case,' the detective told her, 'I think it's time to find and defeat a very dangerous creature, don't you?'

'Definitely,' Nissassa agreed with an icy smile. 'And we may as well kill that nyterra while we're about it, too.' She turned to the jester. 'Which way to the banqueting hall?' she demanded.

'More stairs?' moaned the jester, turning wearily on his heel. 'This way . . . folderol-dee-dee.'

Following behind him, back the way they had come, Clarity turned to Mutt. 'Oh dear, he really isn't very funny, is he?'

A few minutes later, Underduke Ferdinand was alarmed to hear a stomping and a scuffling at the far end of the banqueting hall, followed by a muffled **'Ooomf!'** that sounded suspiciously like a castle guard doubling over after having been hit uncomfortably hard in the stomach.

Duchess Peruka rose to her feet, her face set in a malevolent scowl. The guests around her at the head of the table scraped their chairs back nervously.

There was more disturbance at the far end of the hall. Ferdinand craned his neck to see what was going on.

With a low growl, Duchess Peruka stalked backwards in a crouch, holding up her hands and spreading her fingers like claws. King Bernard's mouth dropped open in shock as he turned to see the duchess preparing to spring at him, looking decidedly murderous. Nearby guests began to stand up and cry out in panic.

'**STOP THE BANQUET!**' came a strident shout from the other end of the hall.

'You have got to be kidding me,' groaned Underduke Ferdinand. And it was at this point that his evil plan really did start to unravel.

He watched in horror as a figure dressed all in black performed a very dramatic flying somersault from the door and landed, with a crash, on the far end of the

banqueting table, causing the assembled nobles and merchants to scramble backwards or, in some cases, to topple over in their chairs, sending several metal platters flying in the process.

Food spattered and splatted in all directions. As the black-clad figure began to sprint down the length of the table, somebody else climbed up behind it. Everybody gasped. Clarity Jones stepped right into the centre of the banquet, her hands on her hips and her face set in a dramatic expression, despite her left foot being in a bowl of soup.

'Don't be alarmed!' she called out to the assembled guests, which was fairly redundant as they were all already *seriously* alarmed. But it seemed like good manners at the time. 'That,' she said, pointing at the growling, crouching non-duchess, 'is not Duchess Peruka! It's a shapeshifting monster called a nyterra!' There were several shrieks of panic at this – most of the guests knew exactly what a nyterra was and had lived in fear of the creature one day returning. 'And it's going to attack the king!' added Clarity for good measure.

The nyterra realized at this precise moment that Underduke Ferdinand was about to be defeated, and decided to take matters into its own claws. With a roar, it began to assume its true form in preparation for its battle with Nissassa, who was still pelting down the table towards it, looking furious and only encountering one brief hold-up when she stepped in a blancmange. And, if the guests at the head of the table had been somewhat shocked when Duchess Peruka had stood up and started growling, they were thrown into complete uproar when she began to expand and split apart, transforming into a hideous, bat-winged monster. The gigantic wig, which the three pole-holding servants had been attempting to keep on her head in an increasingly desperate fashion, toppled over backwards at this point, the candles igniting the wool with an ear-abusing *WHUMPH* and a blast of heat. King Bernard's large ceremonial chair fell over sideways as the nyterra, claws outstretched, leaped through the flames and landed on the table with a piercing shriek of rage.

'Worst. Banquet. Ever,' said one of the merchants to his friend as they stampeded for a side door. But the guards still had orders to let nobody in or out (apart, that is, from the ones who had encountered Nissassa, who had swiftly decided that orders aren't everything). Within seconds, the sides of the hall were a sea of swirling, panicking people. Flames from the burning wig licked high into the air, soon catching on the rich tapestries that hung down from the minstrels' gallery.

As the nyterra prepared for battle and Nissassa launched into another flying somersault, drawing a long, slender sword from a scabbard on her back, King Bernard pulled himself up and squinted down the long banqueting table. He peered through the heat haze at the figure standing, hands on hips, at the other end.

'Clarity?' said the king uncertainly.

'Hey, Dad,' replied Clarity Jones.

And the king's face broke into its first proper smile in nine long years.

THE RUNAWAY PRINCESS

Once upon a time there was a princess. A lost princess. And, just when he needed her the most, her father found her again.

See, told you it got better.

Dodging a selection of panicking merchants, Clarity Jones worked her way down the side of the great banqueting hall of Meandermart Castle, her blue cloak flapping out behind her as she ran. On the table, the nyterra had already abandoned the original plan to attack the king and had turned now to face this new threat – the heavily armed assassin girl sprinting down the table towards it. A great battle was about to begin: Nissassa versus Nyterra.

In its true form, the nyterra was a truly terrifying beast. Seven feet tall, with sharp claws at the end of its powerful arms, it could also attack by balancing on its wing tips and lashing out with its feet, which had hard, pointed toes like spikes. It had no fewer than two rows of teeth in its beak, which was itself razor-sharp. It could attack by flying or jumping on its strong legs . . . Not something you'd want to meet on a dark night, basically. Or even in a quite well-lit setting. And certainly not in the middle of a burning banqueting hall when you'd just stepped in a strawberry-flavoured dessert.

But let's also take a moment to consider Nissassa's abilities. She was Rillia's greatest-ever assassin (semi-retired), a former member of the notorious White Hand Clan. She was an accomplished acrobat as well as an expert at no fewer than seven different forms of hand-to-hand fighting. She'd never been beaten at archery, fencing or axe-throwing and – just to add an extra edge – she was really, really angry with Underduke Ferdinand and the monster who'd been helping him. Clarity Jones had just been falsely accused of a crime and thrown in the cells, and Nissassa was sufficiently interested in the idea of exacting a fairly swift and very painful revenge. So, all things considered, the two combatants were quite evenly matched.

Nissassa vaulted into the air as she approached the nyterra, swooshing her sword threateningly. The beast held up its claws in a defensive motion and the two met with a resounding *CLANG*. And so the great battle was joined, one that the panicking guests bumbling about at the side of the banqueting hall never forgot – much like the guards who'd 'defended' the castle against Mirko.

Nissassa and the nyterra lunged and parried up and down the long table, sending more platters, bowls and goblets flying. The air was full of smoke, heat and fried food. At one point the nyterra spread its wings and took to the air, fanning the flames even more as it lurched up towards the ceiling. But, with a flying leap, Nissassa shimmied up a tapestry and, balancing herself on the edge of the minstrels' gallery, thrust and thrust her sword at the creature as it whirled around, its burning eyes searching ceaselessly for a weakness in her defence.

Clarity Jones, meanwhile, had reached the king, who was standing at the head of the table frozen in

shock. Gently, she pulled him away from the burning tapestries and towards a relatively calm section at the back of the hall. 'This way, Dad,' she told him. 'Don't worry. We've got this under control.'

'Under . . . control?' repeated King Bernard weakly, looking out across the scene of complete and utter chaos that filled the entire chamber.

'Yes,' the lost princess reassured him. 'Me and my friends. We'll protect you. Don't worry.' And somehow, despite the fact that a great deal of the room was on fire, and there was a gigantic bat-like creature that had just tried to kill him engaged in a life-or-death battle with an assassin directly above his head, the king felt better than he had in years.

'Your friends?' he asked his daughter.

'Yes,' she replied, dodging a section of flaming tapestry that was falling from the wall. 'I made some friends on my travels. I'm a detective now, by the way – I'll explain what that is later,' she added quickly, seeing the inevitable question forming on his lips. 'But that's Nissassa,' she went on, pointing proudly to the leather-clad figure above them who had now leaped on to the nyterra's back and was punching it on the side of the head. 'And this is Mutt.'

Mutt had been feeling rather like a spare part since things had turned so very dramatic and climactic battle-y. Not knowing quite what to do, he had followed Clarity Jones down the hall. He'd been startled when she'd called the king 'Dad', and his mouth had dropped open so wide that a flying piece of pie had shot right inside. So at this point he was hovering rather nervously behind the detective, wondering whether it would be entirely heroic if he just hid under the table for a while. It looked nicely sturdy.

When Clarity introduced him to the king, he was so taken aback that he simply said: 'Oh, hello!' and stuck out his hand.

'Hello,' replied King Bernard, who was feeling better by the second. The king shook Mutt's hand enthusiastically.

Underduke Ferdinand, meanwhile, had decided that now would be an excellent time to make a swift and secret exit. While everybody else in the hall was watching the battle taking place above them, he slunk towards the back doors and approached the knot of armoured guards stationed there. 'Let me pass,' he snapped urgently.

'But you said,' recited the guard he'd bullied earlier, 'that nobody gets to leave the room.'

'I wasn't talking about *me*, was I? Obviously!' Ferdinand tutted, panic fluttering in his chest like a trapped bat.

'Oh, so there *was* an exception, was there?' she asked.

'What? Of course there was an exception! *I'm* an exception!'

'Only, you said, "No exceptions." I remember it quite distinctly. I asked several times. "No exceptions." You said it quite clearly. Nobody leaves the room. No exceptions.'

'**Oh, for goodness' sake!**' Ferdinand reached for his belt to draw his sword, but at that moment the door behind the guard was pulled off its hinges to reveal a gigantic shaggy white shape filling the opening.

'Going somewhere, you slimy little toe-rag?' asked the shape.

'Oh, and that's Mirko,' Clarity Jones told her father.

Up on the edge of the minstrels' gallery, the aerial battle was approaching its climax. With a piercing shriek, the nyterra shook Nissassa off its back and flew right up to the wooden beams at the very top of the hall; the assassin landed neatly on the edge of the gallery, balancing on her toes like a dancer. Above her, the monster readied itself for a final, desperate attack. Claws outstretched, it folded its wings tight against its body and plunged downwards, straight towards Nissassa. She readied herself, watching its trajectory intently. Then, at the last possible moment, she launched herself out into nothingness, sword held out in front of her. She timed it perfectly. The nyterra's eyes widened in horror as it realized what was about to happen. But it was too late. Unable to spread its wings quickly enough, its momentum carried it straight on to the point of the assassin's sword, which passed right through it. The monster gave a screech that actually shattered some of the surviving glassware on the table below. And then it plummeted straight down, landing with a resounding CRASH right in the centre of the banquet, the sword sticking out of its chest.

'Kebab, anyone?' said Handy Dandy from the end of the hall.

'Finally,' said Nissassa in a satisfied tone as she

'Detectives,' repeated the duchess slowly. 'Curious word. Yes, if it hadn't been for these detectives, you would have got away with it.'

'I was just thinking exactly the same thing myself,' said Ferdinand, looking at Clarity and her team with an expression of pure, undiluted hatred.

'And what about this boy?' asked Peruka. Mutt felt his face growing hot. He'd come a long way from being Mutt the street dog, but he still wasn't used to hanging out in castles and passing the time of day with kings and duchesses. The fact that Clarity Jones was, in fact, a princess was still blatting around his brain like a pinball. He'd have to process that one later.

'We could never have solved the case without Mutt,' said Nissassa, favouring him with one of her very rare smiles. 'He's the one who didn't eliminate the impossible. He worked out that the last nyterra wasn't dead. If it wasn't for him . . .' There was silence in the throne room as everybody mentally completed that sentence and gave a small internal shudder.

'Hmmm. Yes.' Duchess Peruka looked serious. 'And in the process, you, assassin – you scaled the cliffs and entered my castle without permission. And you, snow gnoblin – you armoured yourself and attacked from the other side, harming several of my guards.'

'Ah yes.' Mirko shuffled his huge furry feet. 'I'm extremely sorry about that, Your Marvellousness. But it was necessary.'

'The penalty for both these crimes is death, you know,' she told them. 'It's the law of Rillia. And I can't change the law.'

'But I can,' said a voice from the throne behind her. King Bernard hadn't felt truly happy in many years. But today he didn't seem to be able to stop himself from smiling. He really wasn't entering into the spirit of Moaningtide even one tiny little bit.

'So, that was lucky,' said Mirko a couple of hours later, as they filed back into the Magical Detective Agency. 'Your father turning out to be the King of Rillia and everything.'

'Yes,' Clarity agreed. 'I knew it would come in useful at some point. I really hated it at the time, though. No mysteries to solve. No adventures. And, worst of all, no pockets.' She swung off her blue cloak as she spoke, hung it on the back of the door and strode over to the fire, which was, as usual, burning merrily in the hearth. She stood there, warming her hands in front of the flames.

Nissassa immediately crossed to the bookcase and, springing the secret catch with the kitten book, began replacing her weapons on their racks in the secret armoury.

Mirko sank into a chair, removing his fearsome helmet and sighing with pleasure. 'That's better,' he said. 'Can't wait to get all this off and run myself a nice bath. I must be filthy under all this metal. Rust stains are a nightmare to shift.'

Mutt, meanwhile, had regained his favourite spot, sitting beside the stone hearth and looking back out across the room that had become a second home.

Smyll came and curled up beside him, immediately falling into a deep sleep on the heathrug, the bottles inside him jangling gently as he snored.

The last two hours had been a blur of excitement and activity, and Mutt's head reeled with tiredness as he tried to put everything in order. He thought about climbing the cliff with Nissassa, finding Clarity, and

storming the banqueting hall, and he thought about the meeting in the throne room afterwards. King Bernard of Rillia had pardoned them all, of course. And now that Duchess Peruka had discovered that the woman calling herself Clarity Jones, Magical Investigator, was actually also the Princess of Rillia, her attitude to the Magical Detective Agency had become considerably friendlier. Especially when she reminded herself that Clarity and her friends had just saved her life. So, before the end of the meeting, the duchess had named the Magical Detective

Agency the first-ever Official Royal Detective Agency, by appointment to the Warden of Meandermart. And after promising to return to the royal castle to spend some proper time catching up with her father and brothers, Clarity had led her team proudly from the throne room to the applause of the assembled courtiers.

'Well then.' Clarity turned to Mutt, with a slight smile on her face. 'What about your trial period, eh? What does the rest of the team think?'

Mirko, who had been carefully unbuckling his gigantic breastplate, halted and waved a rust-stained furry paw in Mutt's direction. 'He was the one who found the jester in the first place, Clarity,' he pointed out.

'Who turned out not to be the real jester at all,' Clarity Jones pointed out in return. She looked serious, but Mutt very much hoped that the sparkle in her eyes meant she was teasing him. 'A misunderstanding which led to my being imprisoned – and those dungeons weren't very nice, you know. I'll be happy if I never eat stew on bread again.'

'You're right, Clarity,' Nissassa broke in, hanging one final dagger – which was called Polly – on its special hook and returning to the main room. 'He also wasted the entire bottle of lie detonator on that monster catcher.'

'What?' Clarity pointed a finger at Mutt. 'You only needed a few drops,' she told him again. 'Any apprentice detective worth his salt would have known that.' Mutt's stomach sank. Perhaps she wasn't teasing him after all.

'So, are you going to take this street dog on as your apprentice or not?' asked Nissassa, straight-faced. 'Remember: we gave him money to spend on boots and he bought a pie instead.'

'Mmm.' Clarity stroked her chin thoughtfully. 'You're right, Nissassa. All things considered, it would be completely impossible for Mutt to join the Magical Detective Agency.'

'What?' Mutt got to his feet, aghast. After all, it had been he who had cracked the case wide open. He'd been the one Smyll had sought out when all had seemed lost. But, just as he was about to let out a stream of very angry words indeed, he noticed the slight smile hovering around Clarity's mouth.

'Yes, completely impossible,' she repeated. 'But, remember . . .'

Nissassa joined her at this point, chiming in at the same time with: 'We never eliminate the impossible!'

'In fact . . .' added Mirko.

'The impossible is our speciality,' finished Clarity Jones, holding out a hand for him to shake.

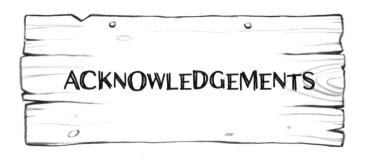

ACKNOWLEDGEMENTS

To everyone at Puffin, but in particular – Super editor Carmen (the impossible is her speciality), Pippa (proof reader/mistake assassin) and Jan (design gnoblin).

Thanks to Kenneth for bringing Meandermart to life with your amazing illustrations.

Enormous thanks to everybody who was kind about *Frankie Best Hates Quests*, especially Cressida Cowell and my elf friend Anna James.

Thanks to Stephanie Thwaites, MA (Magical Agent.)

Thanks as always to Jenny and Lucas, who think it's OK that I make up maps of imaginary places as my actual job.

And to Mabel, for reading through the manuscript alongside me and going 'wow' at appropriate points. I mean she might have been saying 'meow', but it sounded like 'wow', so I'm taking it.

Loved solving mysteries with **Clarity Jones**?

Why not go on a quest with **Frankie Best**?

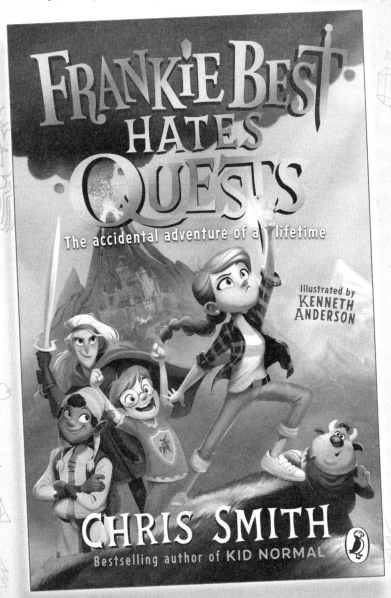

FRANKIE BEST

HATES

QUESTS

The accidental adventure of a lifetime

Illustrated by
KENNETH
ANDERSON

CHRIS SMITH

Bestselling author of KID NORMAL

**From the incredible imagination of
CHRIS SMITH comes an
extraordinary accidental adventure for
fans of Cressida Cowell and Pixar's *Onward*.**

Frankie Best is not happy.

She's stuck at Grandad's with her annoyingly
nerdy brother Joel for a whole week while
her parents swan off to the Arctic.

Then Grandad gets kidnapped, forcing Frankie
to embark on a rescue mission across a
magical realm filled with **strange creatures**,
dangerous **enemies** and – worst of all –
no WiFi!

Frankie did have big plans to watch YouTube
and eat pot noodles that weekend but it
looks like she'll just have to go on an
epic mega-dangerous quest instead . . .

made a delicate landing next to the slain beast, 'the jester says something actually funny.'

'Would someone please explain what on earth is going on?' came a new voice from the end of the hall. And there, in the doorway, stood Duchess Peruka herself – the real one – looking just as confused and startled as any duchess might look after she'd suddenly woken up in a wardrobe.

All things being considered, it was swiftly decided that the Moaningtide banquet would finish early that year. The banqueting hall was on fire, for one thing. For another, a dastardly plot to attack King Bernard had been uncovered and thwarted, and it seemed plain that the treasonous underduke had been behind it. Moreover, most of the food had been trampled underfoot and there was an enormous dead monster in the middle of the dining table with a sword sticking out of it. The guests, it's fair to say, were more than a little keen on the idea of going home. Yes, the signs for continued banqueting at this point were not good.

Instead, Duchess Peruka called a meeting in the

throne room with some people she was extremely keen on hearing from. The first of these was her brother, who attended in chains and surrounded by several guards. The second was King Bernard, who was given the duchess's throne to sit on as a mark of respect and a gesture of apology for having nearly been set upon by a terrifying monster. Handy Dandy was there too, the real one this time, who seemed to have cheered up after his successful joke. And, of course, the members of the Magical Detective Agency were all in attendance. Clarity Jones and Nissassa stood confidently in the centre of the room, with Mutt loitering just behind them, and Mirko was there, once again apologizing profusely to several injured guards on his way in.

'So, let me get this straight,' said the duchess, looking at them steadily. 'You're an assassin.'

'Retired,' added Nissassa.

'And you're a princess.'

'Also retired,' said Clarity Jones with a smile.

'And you,' went on Duchess Peruka, with a glare at her brother, 'are a treacherous little worm. If it hadn't been for these . . . What do you call yourselves again?'

'Detectives,' Clarity told her.